Enid Blyton's CHRISTMAS STORIES

To
Our Special Big Granddaughter
Merry Xmas Lucy! (2016)
lots of love, hugs & kisses
Hope you enjoy the "Xmas
Stories"
from Granny Susan &
Grandad John
XXXX
OOOO

Age 7 - 9 - 10
4 = 7

Also by Enid Blyton

The Famous Five – 21 books, beginning with . . .
Five On a Treasure Island
Five Go Adventuring Again
Five Run Away Together
Five Go to Smuggler's Top
Five Go Off in a Caravan

The Famous Five Colour Short Stories –
8 books, beginning with . . .
Five and a Half Term Adventure
George's Hair is Too Long
A Lazy Afternoon
Good Old Timmy

The Secret Seven – 15 books, beginning with . . .
The Secret Seven
Secret Seven Adventure
Well Done, Secret Seven
Secret Seven On the Trail
Go Ahead, Secret Seven

The Naughtiest Girl – 10 books, beginning with . . .
The Naughtiest Girl in the School
The Naughtiest Girl Again
The Naughtiest Girl is a Monitor
Here's the Naughtiest Girl

Enid Blyton's

CHRISTMAS STORIES

Hodder
Children's
Books

a division of Hachette Children's Group

First published in paperback in Great Britain in 2014
by Hodder Children's Books
This hardback edition first published in Great Britain in 2015
by Hodder Children's Books

A Catalogue record for this book is available from the British Library

ISBN 978 1 444 92846 4

Printed and bound in Great Britain by Clays Ltd, St Ives plc

The paper and board used in this paperback by Hodder Children's Books
are natural recyclable products made from wood grown in sustainable forests.
The manufacturing processes conform to the environmental regulations
of the country of origin.

Hodder Children's Books
An imprint of Hachette Children's Group
Part of Hodder & Stoughton
50 Carmelite House, Victoria Embankment,
London, EC4Y 0DZ
An Hachette UK company

www.hodderchildrens.co.uk

Contents

Introduction

Enid Blyton (1897–1968) wrote over six hundred books in her lifetime and remains one of the world's favourite writers for children. Some of her best-loved stories are about the Famous Five, the Secret Seven and the Naughtiest Girl. She wrote about all kinds of things – about life at school, holiday adventures, fantasy stories about made-up creatures, and animal stories. And *many* stories about Christmas.

Here is a selection of some of her best Christmas stories. You can also read one long story about a family's preparations for the festive season, chapter by chapter throughout the book, which tells you how many popular Christmas customs came to be.

Enjoy the stories – and merry Christmas!

Christmas Holidays

A Family Christmas
Part One:

Christmas Holidays

'HURRAH! CHRISTMAS holidays at last!' said Susan, running into the house joyfully. She was just back from boarding school with her brother Benny, who had broken up the same day.

He came into the house behind her, carrying a heavy bag. His mother was paying the taxi outside. Benny set down the bag, and gave a yell.

'Ann! Peter! Where are you? We're back!'

Ann and Peter were the younger brother and sister still at home. They came tearing down the stairs and flung themselves on Benny and Susan.

'Oh! Welcome back! You're earlier than we expected! Do you know we're going to the pantomime

3

on Boxing Day?'

'Are there any Christmas cards for us?' said Susan. 'Have any come yet? Ooooh – I do love Christmas time.'

'Yes – the Christmas holidays are the best of all,' said Benny, going off to help his mother with more luggage. 'Presents – and puddings – and stockings – and cards – and Christmas trees – and pantomimes – it's a lovely time!'

'There are lots of cards already,' said Peter. 'We haven't opened yours, Susan, or Benny's. And Mum's ordered a fine Christmas tree – and we've stirred the Christmas pudding, and wished. It's a pity you weren't here to wish too.'

'You haven't got any decorations up yet,' said Susan, looking round. 'I'm glad. I do so like to help with those. I don't like you to begin Christmas customs without me here. I like to share in them all.'

'That's why we waited!' said Ann, jumping up and down. 'We wanted you and Benny to share. What fun we shall have!'

The luggage was brought in and taken up to the children's bedrooms. Susan went once more into the room she shared with little Ann, and Benny ran into the one he shared with Peter. How good it was to be home again – and with Christmas to look forward to.

The children unpacked, and their mother sorted out their clothes, some to be washed, some to be put away, some to be mended. They all talked at once at the tops of their voices.

Their mother laughed. 'How any of you can hear what the others say when you don't stop talking for one moment, I can't think!' she said. 'But it's nice to hear you all. Benny, *what* has happened to this sock? It doesn't seem to have any foot.'

'Benny won't hang *that* up on Christmas Eve,' said Ann, with a little giggle.

'He won't hang his stocking up any more, surely?' said their mother. 'He's too big. After all, he's ten now.'

'Well, I'm going to,' said Benny, firmly. 'I don't see why I shouldn't, just because I'm ten. It doesn't matter whether I believe in Santa Claus or not, I can still hang up my stocking, and I know it will be filled. So there, Mummy!'

'All right, Benny, you hang it up,' said his mother, still wondering how it was that Benny's sock had no foot. 'It's nice to keep up these old Christmas customs. There are such a lot of them.'

'There are, aren't there?' said Susan. 'I wonder how they all began. Mummy, why do we hang up our stockings – who first thought of that?'

'I really don't know,' said Mother.

'And why do we put up holly and mistletoe?' said Ann. 'Holly's so prickly – it's a silly thing to put up really, I think. And why do we kiss under the mistletoe?'

'Oh dear – I don't really know,' said Mother. 'These customs are so very very old – goodness knows how they began!'

'Well, I know how Christmas began,' said Ann. 'It's the birthday of the little Christ. Mummy, are you going to tell us the Christmas story, as you always do, on Christmas Eve?'

'Would you like me to?' said Mother.

'Oh *yes*!' said all the children at once.

'Mum, that's one of *our* customs,' said Susan. 'It's not a very old one, not nearly as old as the customs we keep at Christmas time – but it's a very nice family custom of ours, so we'll go on with it.'

'And we'll choose carols and sing them too,' said Ann. 'I like carols better than hymns – they are much merrier, aren't they?'

'Very well,' said Mother. 'We will keep up our family custom this Christmas as usual – carols on Christmas Eve, and the Christmas story.'

'And then off to bed and to sleep, whilst Santa Claus comes down the chimney, very secretly and quietly, to leave his presents!' said Ann.

'It's funny he should hate to be seen giving his presents,' said Peter. 'We are always supposed to be asleep when he comes. Mummy, who was Santa Claus, really?'

'Well – I really don't know,' said Mother. 'What a lot of questions you ask me today. I keep saying "I don't know, I don't know." Do ask me a question I can answer now.'

'Well – why is Christmas pudding called *plum* pudding?' asked Benny, at once. 'There aren't any plums in it.'

'I don't know that either,' said Mother.

'And what is the Yule log?' said Susan. 'I am always hearing about Yule-tide and the Yule log, but I never know exactly what Yule means.'

'Neither do I, really, except that it is another name for Christmas-time. You'd better ask Daddy all these questions when he comes home.'

Now the trunks were unpacked, and were put up into the loft for four whole weeks. It was tea-time, and the children rushed downstairs to a lovely tea. Their mother always had a special cake for the first day the children came home, and special biscuits.

'I love the first few hours at home,' said Susan. 'It's all so deliciously new and exciting – then it gradually gets nice and familiar and homey. Mummy, when are we going to begin the decorating?'

'Tomorrow, if you like,' said Mother. 'Our holly trees in the garden are full of berries this year – and the farmer has said you may go to the big oak trees in his field and cut some mistletoe for yourselves, if you like.'

'But why should we go to the *oak* trees for mistletoe?' said Ann, in wonder. 'Doesn't mistletoe grow on its own bush or tree?'

The others shouted with laughter. 'There *isn't* a mistletoe tree,' said Benny. 'It only grows on other trees – oak trees, for instance, and apple trees.'

'How funny,' said Ann. 'I'd like to see it.'

'You shall, tomorrow,' said Mother. 'Benny shall

take you to the farmer's field, and he can climb up and cut some mistletoe and throw it down for you.'

'We'll cut holly too, and bring stacks of it in,' said Susan. 'And we'll make some paper-chains, and get out the silver stars and bells we had last year, to hang down from the ceiling. Oh, we *shall* have fun!'

'And what about the ornaments for the Christmas tree?' said Benny. 'We'll get those, too. I hope there won't be many broken, they're so pretty and shiny.'

'We'll find the big silver star that goes at the very top of the tree,' said Susan, 'and we'll get out the little old fairy doll and put her under it. Mummy, isn't Christmas time lovely?'

'It is,' said Mother. 'Well, you children will have plenty to do these few days before Christmas, if you are going to do the decorating of the house, the dressing of the Christmas tree, the sending of cards, and the buying of presents.'

'You'll be busy too, won't you, Mum?' said Ann. 'You said you must boil the pudding again – and make

the Christmas cake – and buy some crackers for us –
and finish making some of your presents.'

They finished their tea, and then they heard the
sound of a key being put into the front door.

'It's Daddy!' cried Susan and Benny and they
rushed to welcome him.

'Well, well, you've grown again!' said Daddy,
hugging them both. 'Have you got good school
reports? Who's going to help with the decorating
tomorrow? I've got the day off, so I can take you all
out to get holly and mistletoe!'

'Oh, lovely!' cried Susan. 'Yes, we've got good
reports. I'm top of my form. Oh Daddy, it's lovely to
be home for Christmas!'

'Yes – Christmas is a proper family time,' said
Daddy, hanging up his hat. 'All the old customs to
keep up, the old carols to sing, the old tales to tell!'

'Well, I hope you know a lot about the old customs,
Dick,' said Mother, kissing him. 'These children have
been pestering me with Christmas questions, and I

can't seem to answer any of them.'

'I don't feel like a lot of questions tonight,' said Daddy. 'Tomorrow, perhaps.'

And with that promise they settled down again. They all felt very happy. They were home together, beneath one roof. It would soon be Christmas, the season of goodwill, good cheer, and kindness.

'Christ-mas,' said Susan, separating the two syllables. 'I suppose it means Mass of Christ. What does "mass" mean, in the word Christmas, Daddy?'

'Feast or holiday,' said Daddy. 'The Feast of Christ, a holiday in His honour. There is Michael-mas, too, and Candle-mas.'

'Christ-mas is the nicest time of all,' said Susan. 'People in olden times thought so too, didn't they, Daddy, and feasted and made a holiday?'

'They certainly did,' said Daddy, 'but I am sure they were not happier then we shall be this Christmas-tide.'

The Lost Presents

The Lost Presents

DAN HAD made a present for everybody. He had carved a top for Daisy, a pipe-rack for his father, a table napkin ring for his mother, and he had made a jigsaw puzzle for Auntie because she liked them so much.

'I shall hide them away in a very safe place,' he said, when he had wrapped them all up in Christmas paper and tied them with sparkling string. So he put them in an empty hat box at the bottom of the cupboard in the spare room. Nobody went there. It was a very safe place.

But do you know, when Christmas Eve came and

Daisy began to sort out her presents to put on the Christmas table the next morning, Dan couldn't remember where he had hidden his! He hunted all over the house for them.

'That forgettery of yours!' said Daisy. 'You just can't remember anything, Dan.'

Dan was very sad. 'Now I shan't be able to give anyone anything,' he said. 'I do feel unhappy.'

Well, will you believe it, in the very middle of Christmas night, when he and Daisy were in bed, Dan woke up and remembered where he had put the presents. 'Oh, in the hatbox in the spare room cupboard, of course,' he said, and he got out of bed. Daisy was fast asleep.

Dan looked at their stockings on the end of their beds. They were empty. Father Christmas hadn't come yet. He went creeping along the passage to the spare room. He shut the door so that nobody should see him getting his precious presents.

Yes, there they all were in the hatbox. He counted

them, read the labels, and felt each one to make sure the presents were inside.

Then he crept back to his bedroom and will you believe it, when he got back his stocking and Daisy's were full!

'Well!' said Dan, in delight. 'Father Christmas must only just have gone. I almost met him. Oh, I do feel pleased. I almost met Father Christmas, and I've found all my presents again, so I'm happy!'

Santa Claus
Gets a Shock

Santa Claus
Gets a Shock

It was Christmas Eve. Betty and Fred were in bed, talking quietly. Mother had tucked them up and said good night a long time ago.

'We shall hear quite well if Santa Claus lands on our roof,' said Betty, 'because our house is a bungalow, and the roof is very low. Shall we listen for him, Fred? It's getting near midnight.'

'Yes, let's,' said Fred. 'I'd love to hear him come. We shall hear the reindeer hooves on the roof quite easily!'

So they lay and listened – and do you know, in a

few minutes they heard the sound of sleigh-bells ringing in the distance!

Both children sat up in bed in excitement. 'Do you hear that, Betty?' said Fred. 'It's Santa Claus! Now we'll hear the reindeer on the roof!'

But they didn't! The bells came nearer and nearer, and then stopped except for a tinkle now and then.

'That's funny,' said Fred. 'Santa Claus didn't land on the roof to come down our chimney.'

'Well, where did he land then?' said Betty. 'He must have landed somewhere! I hope he didn't try to land on the garden shed or the greenhouse!'

'We should have heard the tinkle of breaking glass if he'd tried to land on the greenhouse roof,' said Fred with a giggle.

Just then they did hear the sound of something breaking – but it didn't sound like glass. They wondered whatever it could be. They sat and listened. Then they heard the sound of bells again, rather soft – and suddenly there came the noise of a very soft thudding at the window.

'Goodness! Do you suppose it's Santa Claus trying to come in at the window?' said Betty, excited. 'You open it, Fred – hurry!'

The soft thudding came again – knock-knock-knock! Fred slipped out of bed and ran to the window. He drew back the curtain and opened the window.

And whatever do you suppose was poked in at the open window? Guess! It was the long soft nose of a brown reindeer! Yes, in came the nose, and nuzzled up to Fred.

Then beside the first long nose came another – and another and another! Four large-eyed reindeer looked in at that window!

'It was their noses we heard knocking on the window-pane!' cried Betty. 'What do they want? Is Santa Claus there?'

'No,' said Fred, puzzled, peering out of the window. One of the reindeer plucked hold of the little boy's pyjama sleeve and began to pull him gently.

'Let go!' said Fred in surprise. 'You'll pull me out of the window.'

'That's what he wants to do, Fred,' said Betty, watching. 'Look – here's your dressing-gown and your shoes. Put them on, and I'll put mine on too. I think the reindeer have come to fetch us for something.'

As soon as the four reindeer saw the children putting on their clothes, they stopped pulling at Fred's sleeve. They stood patiently at the window, waiting, their bells tinkling very softly as they moved now and again.

The children climbed out of the window on to the grass outside. They had both got their torches, and they flashed them on to see where Santa Claus was.

And what do *you* think had happened to poor old Santa Claus? He had gone across the garden with his big sack of toys, and had walked right over the thinly-frozen pond, without knowing it was there – and the ice had broken, and into the pond had tumbled Santa Claus, toys and all! The reindeer had seen him and come to Fred and Betty for help.

The pond was large and deep. As soon as Fred saw what had happened, he ran to the garden shed. He got a rope from there and threw it to Santa Claus. Then very carefully he and Betty dragged out the poor, wet old man!

'Oh, Santa Claus! What a shame that you should have fallen into our pond!' said Betty. 'You must be so cold and wet! Why didn't you land on our roof?'

'Well, your house is a small bungalow and I never land on bungalow roofs,' said Santa Claus. 'I'm too easily seen from the road if I do – so I usually land in the garden then. Is there anywhere that I can dry myself?'

'We've a fire in the kitchen,' said Fred. 'Everyone is in bed and asleep, so come along and get dry. Aren't your reindeer clever to come and fetch us to help you, Santa!'

The children took Santa Claus into their bedroom and then led the way quietly to the kitchen. There was a nice fire there. Tibs, the cat, was sitting by it. She seemed delighted to see Santa Claus.

'Hello! There's the cat I brought you for a present last year when she was a kitten!' said Santa. 'I remember that she wouldn't stay in your stocking, Betty! Hello, Puss! You've grown into a nice cat!'

Betty made up the fire, feeling really excited. The little girl got a saucepan and poured some milk in it to put on the stove to heat for poor, cold Santa Claus. He took off his wet coat and boots, and did his best to squeeze the water out of his trousers.

'Ah! I shall soon be dry in front of this nice hot fire,' he said. 'Well, it's kind of you children to rescue me! My goodness! I didn't want to spend the night in your pond, I can tell you.'

'Tell us a story, Santa Claus,' begged Betty. So the jolly old chap began to tell the two children how all the toys were made in his enormous castle.

'And, you know, even when the toys are made, they still are not ready to go with me,' said Santa. 'The teddy bears have to be taught to growl – and you wouldn't believe how stupid some of them are! Do you know, I had a bear last year who would keep thinking he was a duck – and every time I pressed his tummy he said, "Quack, quack!"

The children laughed. 'I do wish you'd given him to us,' said Fred. 'He would have made us laugh. Tell us some more, Santa Claus.'

'Well, another time I had a doll that we had to teach to open and shut her eyes,' said Santa, turning himself round so that the fire might dry his back. 'And do you know, she *would* wrinkle her nose and screw up her mouth every time she opened and shut her eyes. So we couldn't give her to anybody either! Fancy having a doll that did that!'

'I think she sounds lovely,' said Betty, imagining a doll that wrinkled her little nose and screwed up her rosebud mouth.

'And another time I had a . . .' began Santa Claus – and then he suddenly stopped and listened. There was a noise at the kitchen door. He went and opened the door – and in walked the four reindeer, dragging the sleigh behind them!

'Oh no! Oh no!' said Santa, trying to push them out. 'You can wait for me outside. How dare you walk in here as if it was your stable!'

The children laughed loudly. It was so funny to see Santa pushing the reindeer on the noses, making them go out backwards, their bells jingling. But they had forgotten that their father and mother were asleep in their bedroom not far off!

And suddenly they heard the sound of their mother's light being switched on. 'That's mother waking up!' said Fred, in a fright. 'Quick, drink up your milk, Santa! Mother may see you. We'll have to pop back to bed!'

Santa drank up the hot milk, snatched up his clothes and his sack, and disappeared into the garden. The children ran to go to their bedroom – but their mother came into the kitchen before they could escape.

'Betty! Fred! How very naughty of you! And you have been heating milk for yourselves too! I suppose you thought you would see Santa Claus if you waited up so late. Really, it's very naughty of you. Anyway, there isn't such a person as Santa Claus!'

'Oh, Mother, there is! He's just been here,' said Fred. 'We heated the milk for *him*. He fell into our pond and got so wet.'

'Don't tell naughty stories,' said Mother, really cross with them.

'Well, Mother, can't you hear the sleigh-bells?' said Betty. She heard them quite clearly as Santa Claus galloped off. 'Oh, Mother, I wish you hadn't come in quite so soon – because now Santa Claus has galloped away without leaving us any presents!'

Mother hustled them into bed and tucked them up again. The children were sad. They were very tired too, and in a few moments they were asleep.

And do you know, in the morning they found two very peculiar toys sitting on the end of their beds! One was a teddy bear that said 'Quack, quack!' instead of growling, and the other was a doll who wrinkled her nose and screwed up her mouth whenever she shut and opened her eyes!

'So it *couldn't* have been a dream!' said Betty, hugging her doll. 'Oh, Fred – aren't we lucky?'

I think they *were* lucky, don't you?

Bringing Home
the Holly

A Family Christmas
Part Two:

Bringing Home the Holly

THE FIRST day of the holidays was sunny and bright. Frost had come in the night, and the grass outside was white and crisp – good to walk on. The children looked out of the window, and longed to be out in the sun, cutting the holly.

'It's lovely that Daddy's got the day off today,' said Susan. 'He's such fun to be with and he's not like some fathers I know. He really talks to us!'

After breakfast they all put on hats and coats, and went out into the garden. Daddy, Benny and Susan had sharp knives for cutting holly sprays. Peter and Ann were to set the cut sprays neatly together on the grass, ready for taking indoors. Then they would all help in putting them up.

'Now, you two take those thick tall bushes,' said Daddy to Benny and Susan. 'I'll have to get the ladder to go up this tree. I'll cut some beautiful sprays from it. Aren't the berries lovely and thick this year?'

'Yes – and what a lovely scarlet!' said Susan. 'Daddy, why do you put up holly at Christmas time! Does holly mean holy tree?'

'Yes,' said Daddy. 'It's been used for so many, many years as a decoration in our churches, you see. There are quite a number of legends about it. I'll tell you some when we have finished cutting, and are having a bit of a rest and a cup of cocoa at eleven o'clock. But I can't talk and cut holly at the same time.'

Daddy fetched the ladder and went up the tree. Soon big sprays of the prickly branches were falling to the ground, and Ann and Peter were kept very busy picking them up.

'They *are* spiny!' said Ann, in dismay. 'Look, this leaf has made my finger bleed, Peter.'

Peter looked. 'It's nothing,' he said. 'I say, Ann, that little drop of blood on your finger is just the colour of the holly berry, look!'

So it was – as brilliant a scarlet as the gleaming berries. Ann wiped away the blood, and went to fetch her gloves. Then she wouldn't feel the pricks so much.

Susan and Benny worked hard at their bushes. Daddy had shown them how to cut out sprays from the very thickest part, so that they would not spoil the shape of the trees.

Ann and Peter ran in and out of the house with the berried sprays. At eleven o'clock Mummy came out with a tray. On it was an enormous jug of cocoa, and a plate of biscuits.

'Oooh, lovely!' said Ann. 'Where shall we have it?'

'In the summer-house,' said Susan. So the tray was

taken there, for it was a nice day. Susan poured out the cocoa. Daddy climbed down his ladder, and came to join them. He had a bright spray of holly stuck into his coat.

'That's for the Christmas pudding,' he said. 'It's such a thickly berried little spray.'

'I like holly,' said Benny. 'Its leaves are so smooth and shiny, and the berries are so brilliant. Daddy, the birds don't go for holly berries nearly as quickly as they go for other berries, do they?'

'No, they don't,' said Daddy. 'They are not so nice – and if *you* ate them, they would make you terribly sick.'

'Is the holly berry like a gooseberry?' said Ann, squeezing one.

'Open one and see,' said Daddy. 'They are not like them at all. They have four tiny "stones" inside, containing the seed.'

'So they have,' said Anne. 'Daddy, why are the leaves so spiny?'

'Well, you could think of that for yourself,' said Daddy. 'Spines or thorns are nearly always grown by plants to prevent themselves being eaten.'

'That holly tree you have been cutting has smooth-edged leaves right at its top,' said Susan. 'There are no spines at all on the top branches, Daddy.'

'Well, there is no fear of a cow or horse having a long enough neck to reach right up to the top!' said Daddy. 'So spines often don't grow on the leaves higher up. Now – what was it you were asking me before, about the holly?'

'You said you would tell us some old tales about the holly,' said Susan. 'Daddy, was holly first used as a decoration when Jesus was born?'

'Oh no,' said Daddy. 'Holly was used long before that. Years before, the Roman people used to hold a great feast at this time of year, the feast of their god Saturn, and they decked his temples with the holly, as well as with other evergreens.'

'Why did they use evergreens?' asked Ann. 'Just

because they were green?'

'People of olden times had a strange belief,' said Daddy. 'They thought, you see, that there were many gods and goddesses living in the woods and in the hills among the trees and bushes. Well, when the wintry weather came, they thought these gods would be cold. So they brought evergreen boughs into their houses and temples, thinking that the forest gods and goddesses would be able to come with them, and nestle in the greenery to escape the bitter frosts outside.'

'Oh,' said Benny, 'what a strange idea. Did the old folk long ago hang up sprays just as we do?'

'They often made them into long festoons,' said Daddy, 'and they sometimes used fruit, leaves, flowers and grain to make their festoons. We too use festoons, but ours are made of paper – your paper-chains, for instance.'

'We are doing what people did hundreds and hundreds of years ago then, when we hang up our paper-chains, for our festoons, and put up evergreens,' said Susan. 'Do you know anything else about the holly, Daddy?'

'Well, there are curious old tales or legends about it,' said Daddy. 'One is that the crown of thorns that Christ was made to wear, was of holly, and that the blood the thorns caused, made the berries scarlet.'

Ann remembered how scarlet her blood had gleamed when she had pricked it with the holly. She was sad when she thought of such a cruel crown for Jesus.

'Another old tale tells about the robin and how he got his red breast,' said Daddy.

'How did he?' asked Peter, looking at a robin who had flown down nearby, hoping for a crumb or two.

'Well, a robin saw Jesus on the cross,' said Daddy, 'and he noticed his crown of thorns. The little bird saw how the thorns pricked Christ's brow, and he flew down to try and peck them out. He stained his breast in the blood of Jesus, and made it red – and, as you see, it is still red to this day.'

'That's a nice old legend,' said Susan. 'I can quite well imagine a robin doing a thing like that, Daddy – they are such friendly little creatures, aren't they?'

'Yes, they are,' said her father. 'I suppose that is why we put them on Christmas cards. Also because they are still with us at Christmas time. They seem to suit the kindly, friendly spirit of Christmas time.'

'Here's a big crumb for you, robin red-breast,' called Ann, and threw out a bit of biscuit. The robin flew down to it, gave a little creamy carol, picked it up and flew off with it.

'I love his rich little voice,' said Susan. 'Well, Daddy – shall we go back to the holy tree, now, to "Christ's thorn," and cut a few more sprays for decoration?'

'We will,' said Daddy, and up they all got, leaving the summer-house to the little robin, who at once flew down and perched on the handle of the empty cocoa-jug.

Soon they had finished cutting the holly, and they took it into the house to put up.

'A big bunch over the doorway please,' said Mother.

'That's where the old, old folk used to hang evergreens,' said Daddy, laughing. 'Here you are – here's a lovely bunch for the doorway.'

'I'll decorate the pictures in the hall,' said Susan. 'Ann, you go up to the bedrooms with these little sprays and do your share there.'

'And here's a beautiful piece for the pudding,' said Daddy, taking the little berried spray from his coat.

'How lovely the holly looks, shining brightly all round the rooms!' said Mother. 'Now – what about some mistletoe? You had better get that after dinner. There's not enough time now.'

'Right,' said everyone. And after dinner off they trooped to get the mistletoe.

A Week
Before Christmas

A Week Before Christmas

THE JAMESON family were making their Christmas plans. They sat round the table under the lamp, four of them – Mother, Ronnie, Ellen and Betsy. Daddy was far away across the sea, and wouldn't be home for Christmas.

'Now, we haven't got much money,' said Mother, 'so we must spend it carefully this Christmas. We can't afford a turkey, but I can get a nice fat chicken. I've made a fine big plum-pudding, and I shall buy as much fruit as I can for you. Perhaps I can buy tangerines for a treat!'

'Can we afford a little Christmas tree?' asked Betsy.

She was ten and loved a Christmas tree hung with all kinds of shiny things. 'Just a little one, Mother, if we can't afford a big one.'

'Yes, I'll see what I can do,' said Mother, writing it down on her list. 'And I've made the cake, a nice big one. I've only got to ice it and put Christmassy figures on it. I'll see if I can buy a little red Father Christmas for the middle of it.'

She wrote down, 'Little Father Christmas,' and then wrote something else down below. 'What have you written?' asked Betsy, trying to see. But her mother covered up the words.

'No – I'm writing down what you three want for Christmas! It's not really a secret because you've all told me – and I shall try my hardest to get them.'

Betsy wanted a big doll. She had never had a really big one, though she was ten. She knew she was getting a bit old for dolls now, but she did so love them, and longed to have a big one before she really *was* too old.

Ronnie wanted a box of aeroplane parts so that he could make a model aeroplane. He had seen one in a shop and longed for it. It would be marvellous to put all the parts together, and at last have a fine model aeroplane that he could take to school and fly for all the boys to see.

Ellen wanted a proper work-basket, one she could keep all her bits of sewing in, and her cottons and scissors and needles too. She was a very good little needlewoman for fourteen years old.

'They're all rather expensive presents,' said Ellen to Ronnie and Betsy, when they had discussed what they wanted. 'We mustn't mind if Mother can't get them. But she did say we must tell her what we really wanted. I know what *she* wants – a new handbag. They're expensive too, but if we all put our money together we might be able to buy her the red one we saw the other day – it's thirty shillings.'

So they made their Christmas plans, and discussed everything together. Since their father had been away

Mother had always talked over everything with the children. They knew she hadn't a great deal of money, and they helped her all they could.

'Tomorrow I'm going to go out and do my Christmas shopping,' Mother said. 'I've got to deliver all the parish magazines for the vicar, too, because his sister who usually does it is ill. I'll do that first, then I'll go and order the chicken and the fruit and sweets – and perhaps some crackers if they're not too expensive. And I'll see if I can buy your presents too – so nobody must come with me!'

'I'll help with the magazines,' said Ronnie. But Mother shook her head.

'No – you break up tomorrow, and there will be plenty for you to do. You're one of the boys that has promised to go back in the afternoon and help to clean up the school, aren't you?'

'Yes,' said Ronnie. His mother was proud of him because whenever there was a job to be done Ronnie always offered to help. 'But I'll be back in good time for tea, Mother.'

The girls broke up the next day too. Then there would be six days till Christmas – days to decorate the house with holly from the woods, to make paper chains to go round the walls, to dress the Christmas tree, paint Christmas cards, and do all the jolly things that have to be done before Christmas Day.

'Ellen, you put the kettle on for tea and lay the table, because I shall be a bit late coming back from my shopping this afternoon,' said Mother, the next day, just after dinner. 'I'll try not to be too late – but those magazines take rather a long time to deliver, and I *must* do my shopping afterwards.'

'I'll have tea all ready, Mother,' said Ellen. 'I'll make you some toast!'

Ronnie went off to help at his school. Ellen sat down to draw some Christmas cards. Betsy joined her. The afternoon passed very quickly.

'Do you know, it's snowing very, very hard?' said

Ellen, suddenly. 'Just look at the enormous flakes falling down, Betsy.'

They got up and went to the window. The ground was already thickly covered with snow. 'Good!' said Betsy. 'Snow for Christmas! That always seems right somehow. And we'll have fun with snowballs and making snowmen.'

'Mother won't like shopping much in this blinding snow,' said Ellen. 'Good thing she's got her rubber boots on. I say, isn't it dark, too? I suppose that's the leaden sky. It looks like evening already.'

The snow went on falling all the afternoon. By the time that tea-time came it was very thick on the ground. Ronnie came puffing and blowing in from the street, and shook the snow off his coat. 'My word, it's snowy! If it goes on like this we'll be snowed up in the morning!'

Ellen put the kettle on for tea and began to cut some bread and butter. Betsy laid the table. Then she went to the window to look for her mother. But it was dark now and she could see nothing but big snowflakes falling by the window.

'I wish Mother would come,' she said. 'She *is* late. She'll be awfully tired.'

Mother *was* late. The kettle had boiled over two or three times before she came. She opened the front door and came in rather slowly. Betsy rushed to her to help her to take off her snowy things. Ellen made the tea.

'Poor Mother! You'll be cold and hungry!' she called. Mother didn't say much. She took off her clothes, put them to dry, and then came in to tea. Ronnie looked at her in surprise. She was usually so cheerful. He saw that she looked sad – and yes, it looked as if she had been crying too! He got up quickly and went to her.

'Mother! What's up? Has anything happened?'

'Yes,' said Mother, and sat down in her chair. 'I've lost my bag – with all my Christmas money in! Oh children, I've looked and looked for it everywhere, and I can't find it. I must have dropped it when I was taking the big bundle of magazines round.'

The children stared at her in dismay. '*Mother!* All your money in it! Oh, poor darling, what a dreadful shock!'

They all put their arms round her. She tried to smile at them, but their kindness made tears come suddenly into her eyes. She blinked them away.

'It's my own stupid fault. I should have been more careful. I can't think *how* it happened – and now this thick snow has come and hidden everything. I'll never find it!'

The children looked at one another in despair. If the Christmas money was gone, it meant no chicken – no sweets – no fruit – no presents! Not even a Christmas tree!

'You drink a hot cup of tea, Mother, and you'll feel better,' said Ellen. 'What a shame! Never mind, darling, we shan't worry if we don't have quite such a good Christmas!'

'We've got the cake and pudding anyhow,' said Betsy. 'But, oh dear,' she said secretly to herself, 'I shan't have that doll now – and next year I'll be too old to ask for one.' But she didn't say a word of this out loud, of course. She was much too unselfish for that.

'I'll go out and look for your bag tomorrow morning,' said Ronnie.

'The snow will be so thick by then that you wouldn't be able to see anything – even if you knew where to look!' said his mother. 'I don't mind for myself, children – but it's dreadful to think you three won't be able to have anything nice for Christmas – not even the lovely presents I had planned to give you.'

'Don't bother about that,' said Ronnie. '*We* shan't mind. Come on – let's have tea and forget about it.'

But, of course, they couldn't really forget about it. They pretended to talk cheerfully, but inside they all felt miserable. When Mother went in to see Mrs Peters next door, they began to talk about it.

'We shall have to do something about this,' said Ellen. 'Mother will be awfully unhappy if she can't even buy a chicken for Christmas Day. We must make plans!'

'What plans?' asked Betsy.

'Well – to earn a bit of money ourselves. Even if it's only enough to buy a chicken or a few tangerines, it will be something,' said Ellen.

There was a pause. Then Ronnie spoke suddenly and firmly. 'I know what *I'm* going to do. The chemist's boy is ill and can't deliver medicines for the chemist. I'm going to offer to deliver them till he's better, and he'll pay me a wage. That will be *my* bit of help!'

'Oh Ronnie – what a very good idea!' said Betsy. 'I wish I could be an errand-girl!'

'You're too small,' said Ronnie. 'You can't do anything. Ellen, can you think of anything *you* can do?'

'Yes, I think so,' said Ellen. 'You know Mrs Harris? Well, she wants somebody to take her three little children for walks each afternoon. I could do that. They're dear little children.'

'Oh, good,' said Ronnie. 'Yes, that would bring in a bit of money too. It's a pity Betsy is too small to do anything. She's not bad for her age.'

Betsy felt sad. She didn't like being the only one who couldn't earn anything for Christmas. She wondered and wondered what she could do. She even lay awake in bed that night, wondering. And then, just before she fell asleep, she thought of something.

She remembered an old blind lady who lived in the next street. What was her name? Yes, Mrs Sullivan. Mrs Sullivan had a companion who read to her each afternoon. But the companion had gone away for a week's holiday before Christmas. Had Mrs Sullivan got anyone to read to her for that week?

'I read quite well,' thought Betsy. 'I'm the very best in my class. I even read all the hard words without being bothered by them. I shall go tomorrow and ask Mrs Sullivan if she would like me to read to her.

Then, if she pays me, *I* shall be doing my bit, too.'

She didn't tell the others, in case they laughed at her. But, next morning after breakfast, she went down the snowy street and found Mrs Sullivan's house.

The snow was now very thick. It had snowed all night long, and in places it was as high as Betsy's knees. She liked it. It was fun to clamber through the soft white snow. She knocked at Mrs Sullivan's door.

She felt a bit frightened. Mrs Sullivan was rather a fierce-looking old lady and she wore dark glasses that made her look fiercer still. Suppose she was cross that Betsy should dare to come and ask to read to her?

Then Betsy thought of her mother's lost bag with all its money in it. This was one small way of helping. She couldn't turn back now!

Mrs Sullivan's daily woman opened the door and took Betsy into a little room where a bright fire burned. A big cat sat beside the old lady. The wireless was on, and music flooded the little room. Mrs Sullivan put out her hand, groped round the wireless set, and turned the wireless off.

'Well, it's little Betsy Jameson, isn't it?' she said. 'And what do you want, Betsy?'

'Mrs Sullivan, I heard that your companion is away for a week's holiday,' said Betsy, 'and I didn't know if you'd got anyone to read to you in the afternoons. You see, Mother has lost her bag with all her Christmas money in it, and we're trying to earn a bit to make up – so I thought . . .'

'You thought I might pay you for reading to me, did you?' said Mrs Sullivan. 'Well, I shall have to try you. There's a book somewhere – pick it up and read me a page.'

Betsy found the library book. She began to read in her clear little voice. Mrs Sullivan listened with a smile on her face.

'Yes, you read quite well for your age – ten, aren't you? I shall be pleased to engage you. I will pay you a shilling an hour for reading to me. Come at two o'clock each afternoon, starting today.'

Betsy felt very proud – but a shilling an hour seemed a lot of money just for reading. 'I'd come for sixpence really,' she said. 'I'm not as good as a grown-up at reading.'

'I shall love to have you,' said Mrs Sullivan. 'You won't mind if we don't have reading *all* the time, will you? I mean – it would be nice to talk sometimes, wouldn't it?'

'Oh yes. But you wouldn't want to pay me just for talking,' said Betsy.

'Well, I'll pay you for your *time*,' said Mrs Sullivan. 'Whether it's reading or talking, or just stroking my cat for me, I'll pay you for keeping me company.'

'Thank you very much,' said Betsy, and she stood up. 'I'll come at two o'clock. I won't be late.'

She went home as fast as ever she could, through the snow. She had something to tell the others! Aha! A whole shilling an hour for six days. If Mrs Sullivan kept her for two hours each afternoon, that would be twelve shillings altogether – enough to buy a chicken, surely!

Ronnie and Ellen thought it was marvellous. They had news to tell, too. 'I've got the job at the chemist's,' said Ronnie. 'He asked me a few questions, and rang up my headmaster, and then said I could come till the other boy is well. I've got to deliver medicines from ten to twelve o'clock each morning, and from three to five each afternoon. And he'll tell me if there's anything urgent for the evening.'

'Oh, *good!*' said Ellen. 'Considering you're only twelve, it's jolly fine to get a job as easily as that. You'll have to be careful not to drop any of the bottles.'

'Of course I shall,' said Ronnie, rather indignantly. 'How did you get on with *your* job, Ellen?'

'Well, Mrs Harris was very pleased,' said Ellen. 'She's going to pay me half-a-crown each afternoon for taking all the children out. They're thrilled! I like little children, so I shall enjoy it. Between us we shall get quite a bit of money for Mother.'

'How much is Ronnie earning?' said Betsy.

'Four shillings a day,' said Ronnie. 'Not bad considering it's only a few hours. Four – and Ellen's two-and-six – and Betsy's two shillings – that makes eight-and-six each day to give to Mother. She'll be able to get the chicken and the fruit and the sweets after all.'

'And perhaps a little Christmas tree,' said Betsy, hopefully.

The next thing to be done was to tell Mother what they had arranged. How they hoped she wouldn't say they mustn't. Mother listened without a word. Then she spoke in rather a shaky voice.

'Yes, you can all do your little jobs, bless you. I don't think I mind losing my bag when I know what nice children I've got. I'm proud of you all. The money will certainly help to buy the things you'd have to go without, now I've lost my bag.'

Nobody brought Mother's bag back to her. Ronnie thought that people must be very mean indeed not to take a bag back to the person who lost it. He called at the police station twice to ask if anyone had brought it in. But nobody had.

All the children began their jobs that day. Ronnie went off to the chemist, and listened attentively when Mr Hughes told him about the deliveries. 'The addresses are on the wrappings of each bottle or package,' he said. 'Be sure to deliver at the right house, and whatever you do, don't just push any package through the letter-box, in order to be quick.'

Ronnie set off with a basket of bottles and packages. The snow was very thick indeed, and it was a long job taking all the medicines round. Ronnie was astonished at the number of people who were ill. Most of them were very surprised to see him, but when he told them why he was doing it they all smiled and nodded.

'It's a pity more children don't do things like that,' said Mr George. 'Helping their mothers when things go wrong.'

Ellen got on very well too. The three small Harris children were delighted to see her. John, Mike and Sally all tried to cling to her hand at once. She set off very happily with them through the deep, white snow.

'We'll play snowballing. We'll build a snowman in the park. I'll try and build you a little snow-house,' promised Ellen. They all had a lovely time, and when she brought them back to their mother at tea-time Mrs Harris exclaimed in delight at their rosy faces and happy talk.

'Oh, Ellen, you've given them such a nice time. Here is your half-crown. You'll come again tomorrow, won't you? The children will so look forward to it.'

'I feel sorry you've got to pay me for my afternoon,' said Ellen, feeling quite ashamed of taking the half-crown. 'I've had just as good a time as the children, Mrs Harris. I really have.'

'Just wait a minute – I've been baking whilst you've been out,' said Mrs Harris. 'I've got a cake for you to take home for yourself and that brother and sister of yours – what are their names – Ronnie and Betsy?'

And she gave Ellen a lovely little chocolate cake, wrapped up in paper. Ellen was delighted. How surprised Ronnie and Betsy would be! She thanked Mrs Harris and hurried off home.

She met Betsy at the gate. Betsy's cheeks were red from Mrs Sullivan's bright fire, and from stumbling home through the thick snow. 'Look,' she said, showing Ellen a bright two-shilling piece. 'That's my first wage. And isn't it strange, Ellen, Mrs Sullivan likes just the kind of stories *I* like! We read a most exciting school story for a whole hour!'

Mother smiled at all the cheerful talk. She had got hot toast and butter and honey ready, and the chocolate cake was put in a place of honour on the table. The children sat down hungrily.

'And Mrs Sullivan and I talked a lot,' said Betsy. 'She told me all about when she was a girl – oh, ever so long ago – and I told her about Ronnie and Ellen and you, Mother. And then I had to brush the cat, Jimmy, and change his ribbon, and get him some milk. I really did have a very nice time. I can hardly wait till tomorrow to find out what happens in the story I'm reading to Mrs Sullivan.'

'I bet she chose a story like that because you wouldn't be able to read a grown-up one,' said Ronnie.

'She didn't! She laughed at all the funny bits too,' said Betsy. 'There's a mam'zelle in the book and the girls are always playing tricks on her. We laughed like anything.'

'Mrs Sullivan is very kind,' said Mother. 'Very, very kind. I ought to pay *her* for having you like this.'

'Oh no, Mother – it's a job of work, really it is,' said Betsy, earnestly. 'Mrs Sullivan says it's not easy to be a really good companion, and she says I am. Really she does.'

'You're a lovely little companion,' said Mother. 'Mrs Sullivan is lucky to have you. But I think she knows it. Well, as I have said before – what nice children I have got!'

'Well, we've got a jolly nice mother,' said Ronnie, unexpectedly. 'And what's more, Mother, I once heard the headmaster's wife saying to the Head that she had noticed that all the nicest children were the ones that had the best mothers – so, if you think *we're* nice, you've got yourself to think!'

Everybody laughed. They all felt happy and cosy. It was so nice to help, and to do a job well. Really it didn't seem to matter any more that Mother had lost her bag!

All the children went to their jobs each day, cheerfully and willingly. Mr Hughes the chemist, Mrs Harris, and blind Mrs Sullivan welcomed them and wished there were more children like them. Ronnie broke no bottles, Ellen made the three Harris children happy, and as for Betsy it would be hard to know which of the two, she or Mrs Sullivan, enjoyed themselves the more.

'Jimmy always purrs loudly when he sees me coming,' Betsy said. 'I wish I had a kitten. Jimmy purrs like a boiling kettle. I put a green ribbon on today and it matched his eyes. It's a pity Mrs Sullivan can't see how nice he looks.'

By the time that the day before Christmas came the children had got their mother quite a lot of money. Enough to buy the chicken, the fruit and a box of crackers! Marvellous!

Just as Ronnie was going home on Christmas Eve morning to get dinner, Mrs Toms called him. She lived in a little house in the middle of the village and she was a friend of his mother's.

'Ronnie! Would you have time to sweep away the snow for me before you go the chemist's this afternoon? I did ask a man to come and do it but he hasn't turned up, and I've got my sister and her children coming on Christmas Day tomorrow. I know you're earning money for your mother and I'd be very glad to pay you for the sweeping.'

'No, I'll do it for nothing,' said Ronnie. 'I'd like to. It would be nice to do something for nothing for a change, Mrs Toms. Have you a broom and a spade? If you have I'll come along at two o'clock this afternoon, before I go to Mr Hughes, and clean up your front path for you.'

'You're a kind child,' said Mrs Toms. 'Thank you very much. If you won't let me pay you I shall give you some of our apples and pears for Christmas instead. I had a lot from my garden this year, and I've saved plenty. So you shall have a basketful to take home.'

Christmas was going to be good after all, thought Ronnie as he went home. He was out again just before two and went to Mrs Toms' house. A spade and broom were waiting for him outside the front door. Ronnie took the spade first. How thick and deep the snow was! Except for a little path, it had been untouched for days, and was quite deep.

He began to dig, shovelling the snow away to the side. He worked hard, and soon took off his coat, he felt so hot.

When he got almost up to the front door he dug his

shovel into the snow, and threw aside a great heap. As the snow fell, something dark showed in it. It tumbled to the side with the snow. Ronnie glanced at it.

Then he looked again, more carefully. He dropped his spade and picked up the dark package. It was a brown bag!

'Mrs Toms! I've found Mother's bag!' yelled Ronnie, suddenly, making Mrs Toms almost jump out of her skin. 'Look, it's Mother's bag – buried in the snow outside your front door!'

Mrs Toms came hurrying out. 'My goodness, is it really her bag? Yes, it is. She must have dropped it in the snow when she came delivering magazines some days ago. Would you believe it! And now you've found it! Well, well – what a good thing you're a kind-hearted lad, and came to sweep my snow away for me – or someone else might have found it and stolen it, when the snow melted!'

'I'll just finish this,' said Ronnie, joyfully, 'then maybe I'll have time to rush home and tell Mother before I start delivering medicines. Oh, my word – what a find, I can hardly believe it!'

He rushed home with the bag. Ellen and Betsy were not there; they had gone to their jobs. But Mother was there, and she stared in delight when Ronnie held out the wet bag.

'*Ronnie!* Oh, Ronnie, where *did* you find it? Is my money in it? Oh yes, everything's there, quite safe. Oh, Ronnie, this is wonderful. Just in time for Christmas, too! I shall go shopping this very afternoon, because now I shall be able to buy you all the presents. I thought you would have to go without. It's too good to be true!'

It was a very happy and joyful Christmas for the Jameson family that year. There was plenty to eat after all, and as much fruit and chocolate and sweets as anyone wanted. There was a Christmas tree hung with all kinds of things and topped with a lovely Father Christmas sent home by Betsy from Mrs Sullivan. Mrs Toms sent a basket of apples and pears. Mrs

Harris gave Ellen a big box of chocolates for everyone. And Mr Hughes presented Ronnie with a box of sweet-scented soap for his mother.

'Everybody's so kind,' said Ellen, happily. 'Oh, Mother – this is the loveliest work-basket you've given me. It's as good as a grown-up's one.'

'And my model aeroplane set is *much* better than I expected,' said Ronnie. 'Mother, you've bought me a more expensive one than I said – it'll make a much bigger aeroplane.'

'I shall call my doll Angela Rosemary Caroline Jameson,' said Betsy, hugging an enormous doll. 'She's the biggest doll I've ever seen and the nicest. Oh, Mother – we never thought Christmas would be like this, did we, when you lost your bag?'

'No,' said Mother, who was busy putting all her things from her old handbag into her new red one. 'We didn't. I didn't think I'd have this lovely bag, for instance. I didn't think I'd be able to get all the things you wanted, or any nice things to eat. But you've managed it between you. I'm proud of you. There aren't many children who would do what *you* have done!'

But *you* would, wouldn't you? It's marvellous how a bit of bad luck can be changed into something good if everybody helps!

The Curious Mistletoe

A Family Christmas
Part Three:

The Curious Mistletoe

'I DO think it's funny to see the mistletoe growing so high up, on another tree,' said Ann, puzzled, when she and the others stood, after dinner, in the farmer's field, looking up at a great tuft of mistletoe growing on an oak tree.

'Well, it's what we call a *parasite*,' said Daddy, leaning the tall ladder against the sturdy oak tree.

'What's that?' asked Peter.

'A parasite is something that lives and feeds on something else,' said Daddy, 'it gets its food from its *host*, as we call the plant or animal it lives on.'

'Does the mistletoe find its food in the oak tree

then?' asked Susan. 'How does it?'

'The seed sends down little threads or *sinkers*,' said her father, climbing up the ladder. 'These sink into the branch of the tree, and feed on the sap there. Then up come two rather dingy green leaves, and hey presto! That is the beginning of one of the great tufts of mistletoe you see up here!'

'I'm coming up the ladder too,' said Benny, 'I'll throw down what you cut to the others.'

Daddy had to climb right into the tree to get to the mistletoe. It stuck out of the trunk and branches of the oak in great, bushy tufts. It glistened with pearly berries.

'It's not really very pretty,' said Benny, throwing down a big piece to the others. 'Not nearly so pretty as the holly. Why do we have it for decoration? I suppose there are all kinds of tales about the mistletoe, too.'

'Oh yes,' said Daddy. 'I'll tell you them this evening, after tea. Now – here's a nice bit – catch!'

'We'll hang that up in the front porch,' cried Susan, as it came down to her. 'People always kiss each other under the mistletoe, Daddy, don't they? Do you know why?'

'Well, the mistletoe was dedicated to the goddess of love in the old days,' said Daddy, coming down the ladder, 'so I suppose it was natural to kiss under the mistletoe.'

'What a nice lot we've got,' said Ann, picking up the pearly sprays. 'Does it only grow on oak trees, Daddy?'

'It grows on poplars too,' said her father, 'and on apple trees, hawthorn and lime trees as well. It is only *half* a parasite really, because it has green leaves which do work like the green leaves of other plants. But its sinkers steal sap, as I told you before.'

'Who plants the mistletoe?' said Benny, puzzled. 'And how is it planted? Did the farmer plant it on these trees?'

'Oh no, Benny!' said Daddy, laughing. 'Of course not. The birds plant the mistletoe. The mistle-thrush plants most of it, I suppose.'

'However does it do that?' said Benny, astonished.

'Well, the mistle-thrush is very fond of the mistletoe berries,' said Daddy. 'He feasts on them, and then finds that some of the seeds have stuck to his beak. Squash a mistletoe berry, will you – and see how sticky it is.'

Each of the children squeezed a berry between finger and thumb. 'Gracious! It's as sticky as glue!' said Ann.

'Yes – the seeds are very very sticky,' said Daddy. 'Well, when the thrush finds his beak sticky with them, he flies off to a tree and wipes his beak carefully on a bough to clean it. He probably leaves behind one or two of the sticky seeds. They don't fall off the bough – they stick there tightly.'

'And they grow there!' cried Peter. 'So that's how the mistle-thrush plants them – but he doesn't know it.'

'He certainly doesn't know it,' said Daddy, smiling. 'He flies off with a nice clean beak. The seeds he has left roll stickily down to the under part of the bough, stay there for a while, and then send out their sinker-threads. As soon as they reach the sap in the bough, they are able to feed on it and make leaves – then up grows a mistletoe bush, and when it has its berries, along comes the mistle-thrush and has a feast again!'

'I could plant some mistletoe myself, couldn't I?' said Ann, pressing a seed into a crack on the underside of an oak branch. 'There, sticky seed. Hold on tightly, put out your sinkers, and grow into a mistletoe bush for me, just for me.'

The others laughed. 'I suppose you think that by tomorrow there will be a nice big tuft of mistletoe for you, complete with berries!' said Peter. 'It will take ages to grow, won't it, Daddy?'

'Yes,' said his father, 'but no doubt in a few years there will be a nice little mistletoe plant there for Ann, and she will be very proud to pick it.'

'We've got enough mistletoe now, haven't we?' said

Susan. 'Let's take it indoors. Daddy, did the early Christians use mistletoe? Is that why we put it up at Christmas-time?'

'Oh, mistletoe has been a holy and sacred plant for thousands of years,' said Daddy. 'Long before Jesus Christ was born. Christians took over a great many old customs and used them in their own way. Some of the things we do in our Christian religion were done by pagan peoples centuries before Jesus came – for old customs are difficult to kill.'

'Yes – I suppose it's better to keep to old customs, and give them a new meaning,' said Susan, wisely.

'That's very well put,' said her father, pleased. 'That's exactly what you might say about the mistletoe. Centuries and centuries ago, the Druids, who were the priests of the people of long ago, worshipped the oak tree, and worshipped also the mistletoe that grew on it.'

'Did they really?' said Peter. 'It seems odd to worship trees.'

'Oh people have worshipped and prayed to many odd things,' said Daddy. 'The sun – and the moon – and the stars – trees and animals – all kinds of things, even idols of stone and wood that they themselves have made.'

'Still, it does seem strange to worship a funny plant like mistletoe, just because it grew on the sacred oak,' said Peter. 'I wouldn't have, if I'd lived in those days!'

'Oh yes you would!' said Daddy. 'You believe what you are taught, no matter in what century you live. There are very few people who are strong enough to think out everything for themselves, so nearly all of us believe what we are told to believe, worship what we see other people worshipping, and follow the customs we have known from childhood.'

'Well, anyway I shall find out if I can how all these old customs began,' said Peter, stoutly. 'I don't believe that mistletoe is sacred and ought to be worshipped, but I like to know who first taught that it should be.'

'Quite right,' said Daddy. 'Find out all you can.

Well, as I said, the old priests, the Druids, worshipped the mistletoe because it grew on their sacred tree, the oak. They used to chant songs and carols when they cut sprays to hang up at their festivals – just as we cut it now to hang up at our festival at Christmas-time.'

'Why did the long-ago folk think that they ought to worship the mistletoe, just because it grew on the oak?' wondered Susan.

'Well, one reason was that the oak leaves died in the winter, but the mistletoe on the oak remained green as you see it now,' said Daddy, beginning to walk home again. 'So they said, "Ah, the life of the oak had gone into the mistletoe. The spirit of the oak is in that tuft. We must be careful of it and worship it, for it now contains the life of the sacred oak." Then, when the leaves of the oak grew green again, they said that the life of the oak had gone from the mistletoe back to the tree.'

'What strange ideas,' said Susan. 'Of course we know that the mistletoe is only a half-parasite, planted by a bird – so we don't have those strange ideas.'

'The mistletoe has always been used as a kind of charm by peoples of many countries,' said her father. 'Sometimes it was used for driving away evil spirits. Sometimes the leaves were powdered and scattered over the fields to make crops grow well. Sometimes hunters carried a sprig of it hoping that it would give them success in their hunting!'

'I think *I* shall wear a sprig and see if it brings *me* good luck,' said Ann, at once. She broke off a little spray and stuck it into her hat. 'There. We'll see if the mistletoe is still as lucky as the old folk used to think!'

Everyone laughed. 'Ann *would* do something like that,' said Susan. 'Is the mistletoe supposed to do anything else strange, Daddy?'

'It was supposed to open all locks and doors,' said her father, opening the gate of their garden.

'Oh,' said Peter, 'perhaps it would open my old money-box, Daddy. I've lost the key.'

'Well really!' said Daddy, 'I'm not telling you all these things for you to try out yourselves. I'm only telling you what long-ago, ignorant people believed in the childhood of the world.'

'I know,' said Peter. 'But I'll just *see* if the mistletoe will open that box.'

Mother came to meet them. 'What a long time you have been,' she said.

'Well – we had a lot to talk about,' said Susan. 'Mummy, Daddy knows such a lot about the mistletoe.'

'Well, does he know why we are supposed to hang it from something, instead of putting it behind pictures as we do holly?' said Mother, laughing. 'Can he tell me that? No one has ever told me why.'

'Yes, I can tell you,' said Daddy. 'It once killed a beautiful god, called Balder, and ever since then it has been made to grow high on a tree, out of harm's way. It must not touch the earth or anything on it – so we have to hang it, instead of letting it rest against our walls. Ah – I knew that, you see.'

'Who was Balder?' asked Susan, who was always on the look-out for a story.

'I'll tell you after tea,' said Daddy. 'My voice is getting hoarse from talking so much. Wait till we're sitting round the fire, and I'll tell you.'

The Christmas
Tree Aeroplane

The Christmas Tree Aeroplane

ALL THE children in the village were as excited as could be, because the lady at the Big House was giving a party – and every boy and girl was invited!

'I'm going to wear my new suit!' said Alan.

'I'm going to have on my new blue dress,' said Eileen.

'There's going to be crackers and balloons!' said John.

'And an *enormous* Christmas tree that nearly reaches the ceiling!' said Harry.

'And a lovely tea with jellies and chocolate cake!' said Belinda.

'It will be the loveliest party that ever was!' said Kenneth.

'Look! There's the tree going up to the Big House!' cried Fred. All the children ran into the lane and watched the cart going up the snowy road, with a big Christmas tree lying on it.

'There's a fine pack of toys for this tree!' called the driver, who was Alan's father. 'I've seen them. My, you'll be lucky children!'

'What's for the top of the tree?' asked Belinda. 'Will there be a fairy doll?'

'No, not this year,' said the driver. 'There is something different – it's Santa Claus in an aeroplane! He's going to be at the top of the tree, looking mighty grand in his plane, I can tell you!'

'How lovely!' cried all the children – and they thought that it would be even nicer to have Santa Claus in an aeroplane at the top of the Christmas tree than a fairy doll.

At last the great day came. Everybody was dressed

in their best. Every girl wore new ribbons and every boy had brushed his hair down flat till it shone. They all went up to the Big House as happy as could be.

At least, all of them except Harry. He went with the others, but he didn't feel very happy. His suit wasn't new – it was only his old one, because he hadn't a best one. His shoes wanted mending, and he hadn't even got a clean hanky, because his mother was ill in bed and couldn't see to him properly. But Harry had washed his face and hands, and brushed his hair as well as he possibly could.

He soon forgot about his old suit and his old shoes. The children shouted with joy when they went into the big hall and saw the Christmas tree there. Its candles were not yet lighted, but all the ornaments and presents hung on it, and it looked beautiful.

'Look! There's the aeroplane at the top of the tree!' cried Kenneth. Every one looked – and, dear me, it certainly was a very fine aeroplane. It shone and glittered, and the little Santa Claus inside grinned in a jolly way at all the children.

'I wonder who will have the aeroplane for a present,' said John.

Mrs Lee, the lady who was giving the party, smiled at him. 'Nobody will have the aeroplane,' she said. 'I bought it to go at the top of the tree, not for a present. It is just to make the tree look pretty.'

The party was lovely. There were games of all kinds and there were prizes for those who won the games. Everybody won one except Harry, who really was very unlucky.

Then balloons were given out. Harry got a great big blue one. He was very proud of it. And just as he was throwing it up into the air, playing with it, he heard some one's balloon go pop!

It was little Janey's! She had thrown it by mistake against a spray of prickly holly, and it had burst. Janey burst too – into tears! She sobbed and sobbed – but there was no balloon left for her to have another.

Harry went up to her. 'Have my balloon, Janey,' he

said. 'Here it is. It's a beauty. You have it, and then you won't cry any more.'

Janey was simply delighted. She took the blue balloon and smiled through her tears. 'Oh, thank you, Harry,' she said. 'I do love it!'

Wasn't it nice of Harry? He watched Janey playing with his balloon until tea-time – and then the children sat down to a lovely tea. Oh, the cakes there were! And the dishes of jellies and blancmanges! They really did enjoy themselves!

At the end of tea, Mrs Lee gave each child three crackers. They pulled them with a loud pop-pop-pop! Out came toys and hats.

Harry was unlucky with his crackers. The other children who pulled with him got the toys out of his crackers – and he only got a hat. And that was a bonnet, so he gave it to Ruth.

The next exciting thing that happened was the Christmas tree! All the children went into the hall, and there was the tree lighted up from top to bottom with pink, yellow, blue, green and red candles. It looked like a magic tree.

'Isn't it lovely!' cried all the children. 'Oh, isn't it lovely!'

Then Mrs Lee began to cut the presents off. As she did so, she called out a child's name.

'Kenneth!' And up went Kenneth and took a train.

'Belinda!' And up went Belinda and was handed a beautiful doll.

'Alan!' Up went Alan and had a big fat book of stories. It was so exciting.

But one little boy was left out! It wasn't Harry – he had a ship. It was Paul. For some reason he had been forgotten, and there was no present for him at all. Mrs Lee smiled at all the children and told them to go into the dining-room again to play some more games – and Paul didn't like to say he had had no present from the tree.

'Where's your present, Paul?' asked Harry, as they went into the big dining-room.

'I didn't get one,' said Paul, trying to look as if he didn't mind. 'Perhaps Mrs Lee doesn't like me. I was rather naughty last week, and she may have heard of it.'

'But, Paul, aren't you unhappy because you haven't got anything?' said Harry, who thought Paul was being very brave about it.

'Yes,' said Paul, and he turned away so that Harry shouldn't see how near to crying he was. It was so dreadful to be left out like that.

Harry thought it was dreadful too. He put his arm round Paul. 'Take my ship,' he said. 'I've got one at home. I don't need this, Paul.'

Paul turned round, his face shining. 'Have you really got a ship at home, Harry?' he said. 'Are you sure you don't want it?'

Harry *did* want it – but he saw that Paul wanted it badly, too. So the kind-hearted boy pushed his precious ship into Paul's hands, and then went to join in a game.

When half-past six came, the party was over. Mothers and fathers had come to fetch their children. How they cried out in surprise when they saw the balloons, the cracker-toys, and the lovely presents and prizes that their children had!

Only Harry had none. His mother did not come to fetch him because she was ill. His father was looking after her, so Harry was to walk the long dark way home by himself. It was snowing, so the little boy turned up his collar.

He went to say goodbye and thank you to Mrs Lee. He had good manners, and he knew that at the end of a party or a treat every child should say thank you very much.

'Goodbye, Mrs Lee, and thank you very much for asking me to your nice party,' said Harry politely.

'I'm glad you enjoyed it,' said Mrs Lee, shaking hands with him. 'But wait a minute – you have forgotten your things. Where is your balloon? And your cracker-toys – and your present? You surely don't want to leave them behind.'

Harry went red. He didn't know what to say. But little Janey called out loudly:

'Oh, Mrs Lee, my balloon burst, so Harry gave me his lovely blue one. Here it is!'

'And he only got a bonnet out of one of his crackers, and he couldn't wear it because he's a boy,' said Ruth, holding up the red bonnet. 'So he gave it to me.'

'But where is your present?' asked Mrs Lee. 'I know I gave you a ship!'

'Here's the ship!' said Paul, holding it up. 'He gave it to me.'

'But why did you do that, Harry?' asked Mrs Lee in surprise. 'Didn't you like it?'

'I loved it,' said Harry, going redder and redder. 'But you see, Mrs Lee, Paul didn't get a present. You forgot him. And he really was very brave about it, so I gave him the ship.'

'Well!' said Mrs Lee in astonishment, 'I think you must be the most generous boy I've ever known.

But I *can't* let you go away from my party without *some*thing! Wait a minute and let me see if there is anything left.'

She looked in the balloon box. No balloons. She looked in the cracker boxes. No crackers! She looked on the tree – not a present was left! Only the ornaments were there, shining and glittering.

'Dear me, there doesn't seem to be anything left at all,' said Mrs Lee. And then she caught sight of the beautiful shining aeroplane at the top, with Santa Claus smiling inside. 'Of course! There's that! I didn't mean any one to have it, because it is such a beauty and I wanted it for the next time we had the tree – but you shall have it, Harry, because you deserve it!'

And she got a chair, cut down the lovely aeroplane, and gave it to Harry. He was so excited that he could hardly say thank you. He had got the loveliest thing of all!

The other children crowded round him to see. 'Oooh! Isn't it lovely!' they said. 'How it shines!

And isn't Santa Claus real? You *are* lucky, Harry – but you deserve it.'

'Yes, he deserves it,' said Mrs Lee, smiling. 'And I am going to take him home in my car, because I don't want him to be lost in the snow. Wait for me, Harry!'

So Harry waited, hugging his fine aeroplane and feeling happier than he had ever been in his life. And when Mrs Lee came up with her fur coat on, she carried a box of cakes and a big dish of fruit jelly for Harry's mother.

'I thought I was going home with nothing – and I'm going home with more than anybody else,' said Harry in delight.

'A kind heart always brings its own reward,' said Mrs Lee. 'Remember that, Harry!'

He always does remember it – and we will too, won't we?

Balder the Bright
and Beautiful

A Family Christmas
Part Four:

Balder the Bright and Beautiful

AFTER TEA the children pulled their father's chair near to the fire. Ann fetched his pipe. Peter put his tobacco pouch beside him.

'This is all very touching,' said Daddy, with a laugh. 'I suppose it means that you want the story of Balder.'

'Of course,' said Ann, getting on to his knee. 'You tell stories so nicely, Daddy. Fill your pipe and begin.'

Daddy began to fill his pipe, thinking hard.

'Who *was* Balder?' asked Peter.

'Well,' said Daddy, and he began. 'Here is the story of Balder the Bright and Beautiful . . .

'Once upon a time, so the old Norsemen say, there lived many gods and goddesses, some good and some bad. They lived in the city of Asgard, and they were very powerful. There were great giants in those days too, strong and mighty, living in the ice country.

'Odin was the chief of the gods, and lovely Frigga was his wife. They sat on their thrones in Valhalla, in the lovely city of Asgard.

'The best-loved god of all was Balder the bright and beautiful. He was Frigga's son, and she loved him dearly. All the gods loved Balder, and the men and women of the earth loved him too, and even the stony giants.

'His face was dazzling to look at, for he was very beautiful, and very kind. To see Balder was like seeing the bright sun, warm and lovely.

'One night Balder had a strange and frightening dream. When he awoke his heart felt heavy. "There is a shadow there," said Balder, and he pressed his hand to his heart. "I must go to my mother, Frigga.

Maybe she will tell me what the shadow is. I have dreamed a dreadful dream, and it has left its shadow behind."

'Balder arose and went to find his mother, Frigga. She sat on her throne, looking out over the heavens. Balder lay down at her feet, sad and gloomy.

'"Balder, what is the matter?" said Frigga, in the greatest surprise, for never before had the god looked so unhappy.

'"Mother, I have a shadow in my heart," said Balder, and he took his mother's hand in his. He pressed it to his heart, and she felt the shadow there. She grew very pale, and stood up in fear.

'"My son, my son!" she said. "It is the shadow of death!"

'"If death comes to me, I will meet it bravely," said Balder; but his bright face shone no more.

'"You shall not die!" said Frigga. "I am the queen, and everything must obey me. I will send word for everything in the earth to come to me, and I will make them promise not to hurt you, Balder, my son. Then, if you cannot be hurt, you cannot be killed."

'Frigga did not waste a moment. She sent out her commands at once. "Tell everything in the earth to come before me," she said. "And, when they are before me, they must swear to me never to hurt Balder the bright and the beautiful."

'Then all things on the earth came to her as she commanded. Every one of them swore an oath never to harm Balder.

'Fire, water, iron and all metals, stones and earth, trees, sicknesses, poisons, beasts, birds and creeping things, all bowed down before Frigga, and promised her what she wanted. Then the Queen of Asgard was happy again, and smiled at Balder her beloved son.

'"You are safe, my son," she told him. "Now nothing can harm you."

'But Balder still felt the heavy shadow in his heart, and was sad. "It will go," said Frigga. "There is nothing that can bring you death."

'The gods soon heard that everything on earth had promised not to hurt Balder. "Does that mean that a spear will not wound him, that a stone will not bruise him?" they said to one another.

'"Even so," said Balder. "You can try to spear me or cut me with your swords, but you cannot hurt me, for they are made of things that have promised my mother, Frigga, never to harm me."

'"Let us play a new game," said the gods. "Let us take Balder to the green that is outside the City of Asgard, and stand him there in the middle of it. Then let us take our weapons and hurl them at Balder. It will be strange to see them fall to the ground without harming him."

'So they took Balder to the green and put him in the middle. He stood there laughing, his face bright once more, for he had forgotten the shadow in his heart in the joy of the game.

'The gods took their great spears, sharp-pointed and strong. One after another they hurled them at Balder. But how strange – every spear glanced away and fell clanging to the ground. Not one would hurt Balder.

'Then the gods took their swords, and they hacked at Balder, who stood laughing there. But not one sword would touch him, for the metal had promised never to harm him. They slipped aside from Balder and no matter how hard the gods tried, they could not cut him with their swords.

'Then they brought out their staves, great sticks of wood, heavy and strong. They struck at Balder with these, but the staves broke in half and would not hurt him.

'"You cannot hurt me," laughed Balder. "You will only tire yourselves."

'But the sport was a good one, and the gods went on with the same game for a long time, laughing and shouting.

'Then a wicked god called Loki heard the shouting and wondered what it was all about. He went near to see. He was amazed when he saw that the gods were trying to spear and cut Balder the bright and the beautiful.

'"Now what is this?" said Loki to the laughing gods. "Do you love Balder no more? You will kill him!"

'"We cannot," said the panting gods. 'Everything has promised Frigga that it will not harm Balder. See, we throw our spears, hack at him with our swords, and strike at him with our staves. But everything keeps its promise to Frigga, and will not hurt him."

'Loki was jealous of the beautiful god Balder. He was jealous of his beauty, and jealous of the love that everyone gave him. He wondered if it were really true that everything had promised not to hurt Balder.

'"I will ask Frigga," he said. But he did not dare to go to the Queen of Asgard as himself, for Frigga did not like Loki. So he dressed himself as an old, old woman and went to the palace where Frigga had her throne.

'Loki came before the kindly Frigga, looking like a poor old woman. Frigga bade her sit down, and they began to talk.

'"Have you come from far?" asked Frigga.

'"Yes," said Loki, "and I saw a strange sight before I entered the gates of Asgard."

'"What was that?" asked Frigga.

'"I saw Balder the bright and beautiful, standing, in the midst of the green," said Loki, "and behold all the gods were hurling their spears and staves at him, but Balder stood there, laughing, unhurt."

'"That is a new sport for the gods," said Frigga, smiling. "Everything has promised me never to hurt my son Balder so it matters not what they throw at him, he cannot be killed."

'"Did you say that *every*thing has promised you, every single thing?" said Loki.

'"Only one thing did not promise," said Frigga. "And that is so small and weak that I did not ask it to. It cannot hurt Balder."

'"What is that one thing?" aked Loki, in a low voice, wondering if Frigga would tell him.

'But Frigga had no idea that this was Loki, the wicked god, in front of her. She merely thought him to be a poor, simple old woman, and she answered him freely.

'"That one thing is the little mistletoe plant. It grows in the palace gardens, and is so small that I did not bother to ask it to promise. How could it hurt my brave son Balder?"

'This was all that Loki wanted to know. With shining eyes he left the Queen of Asgard, and went into the palace gardens. He changed himself back into his own shape and looked about for the mistletoe plant.

'He soon found it, growing small and sturdily in a strong tuft. He cut it, and made a short but very strong stave. Then he hurried to join the gods.

'They were still playing their new game, for they had not yet tired of it. Loki went up to them and watched. He did not dare to hurl the mistletoe stick himself, for surely the gods would all fall upon him in anger if he hurt their beloved Balder. No – someone else must throw the stick.

'He looked round the ring of laughing gods and there saw blind Hodur, the twin brother of Balder. Hodur loved Balder, and was sad that he could not see this new game, nor join in it. Loki went up to him quietly.

'"Would you too like to throw something at Balder?" he said. "You must not be left out. I will put a stick into your hand to throw."

'"I cannot see to throw. You know that well," said Hodur.

'"I can guide your aim," said Loki. "Draw back your arm, Hodur, and hurl the stick with all your might, for it will not hurt Balder. I will guide you."

'Hodur did as Loki said. He drew back his arm, and threw the stick of mistletoe with all his strength. Loki guided his arm and the stick flew straight at Balder.

'It struck him on the heart and pierced it. Balder gave a terrible cry and fell to the earth at once. The gods stared in amazement, puzzled and alarmed. "What is it? Tell me," cried blind Hodur, knowing by his brother's cry that he had been grievously wounded. "Balder, speak to me!"

'But Balder could speak no more. He was dead. The gods lifted him up in horror, weeping for him, and Hodur, stretching out his hands in front to feel his way, tried to go to Balder too.

'The gods went back to the City of Asgard. They came to Valhalla, and saw Frigga there, seated on her throne. How were they to tell her? But she saw their tearful eyes, and she knew that something terrible had happened.

'"Balder the bright and beautiful is dead!" went the whisper round Asgard. "Loki it was that killed him. Balder is dead!"

'Hodur, filled with anger and grief, sought

everywhere for Loki to punish him. But that clever god had slipped away, and no one knew where he hid.

'"How could I have thrown that stave at my beloved brother?" said Hodur, and he wept bitterly. "Why did I not guess that Loki meant to kill him?"

'Balder's body was taken to the seashore. His ship, called *Ringhorn*, was there to take him on his last journey. It was the biggest ship in the world.

'It was the Norse custom to place a dead man on his own ship, then set fire to it, and let the burning ship sail away on the sea. But Ringhorn, Balder's ship, would not move away from the shore.

'"Send for the giantess Hyrrockin," said Odin. "She must push the great ship out to sea for us."

'So a messenger was sent to the giantess, and soon she came riding up on a great wolf.

'"Push my son Balder's ship out to sea," said Odin. So Hyrrockin caught hold of the ship with her two great hands, and pushed it so strongly that it sped down the rollers to the sea, fire flashing beneath it as it went. The whole earth shook as the ship took the sea.

'Blazing high, it floated out on the waves, till it was lost to sight in the coming night. So passed Balder the bright and the beautiful.

'Then Frigga took the mistletoe and planted it high on a tree, so that never again could it touch the earth, and bring harm to anyone. And, to this day, the mistletoe still grows high in the branches of trees.'

There was a pause at the end of the story. No one had interrupted at all. Ann looked rather solemn.

'Oh Daddy – what a lovely story! But I didn't want the mistletoe to kill Balder.'

'I know,' said Daddy, 'but I can't alter the story, I'm afraid.'

All the children looked up at the bunch of mistletoe hanging down from the light, its pearly berries gleaming grey-green.

'We know a lot about you now, Mistletoe!' said Peter. 'What an old, old plant you are, and what an old, old story you have. Next time we kiss under the mistletoe we'll think of your strange history.'

'And now it's time for bed, Ann,' said Mother. 'Tomorrow we'll have a lovely time, decorating the Christmas Tree!'

A Hole in
Santa's Sack

A Hole in
Santa's Sack

ONE CHRISTMAS TIME the green goblins thought it would be a fine idea to follow Santa Claus and cut a hole in his sack. Then, maybe, some toys would fall out and they would have a fine time playing with them.

So they laid their plans, and on Christmas Eve they followed Santa Claus when he dashed through the sky on his sleigh. The bells jingled, and the reindeer tossed their big heads as they galloped over the clouds. Santa Claus sang a rollocking song as he went, and down below people said, 'Dear me, someone's got their television on very loud tonight!'

The green goblins had a small aeroplane, and when

Santa Claus landed on a roof they landed too – but behind a chimney pot so that they shouldn't be seen. They crept out of their plane and peeped to see what Santa was doing. He had put his sack down and was tying his reindeer up to a big chimney.

'Now's our chance,' said the green goblins. 'Who has the scissors?'

'I have,' said the biggest goblin. He ran up to the sack and snipped a hole in it. Then he ran quickly back behind the chimney as Santa Claus turned to pick up his sack. Whistling softly, the jolly old man slipped down the chimney. The goblins heard something fall from his sack as he hoisted it up on his shoulder.

When Santa Claus was safely down the chimney the goblins ran to see what had fallen out. It was a large red box!

'What is it?' cried the goblin. 'Oh, it must be full of toys! How lovely! It must be full of toys!'

They popped the box behind a chimney and waited for Santa Claus to come up again. They thought maybe he would drop something else out of the hole in his sack. But what a disappointment for them! When old Santa came up from the chimney the goblins saw that he had found the hole and had pinned it up with a large safety-pin!

Santa Claus spoke crossly to his reindeer.

'Do you know, I found a big hole in my sack just now, reindeer? I've told you before that you are not to nibble my sack!'

Then he got into his sleigh and drove away. The green goblins looked at one another.

'It's no good going after him now,' said the biggest one. 'He won't drop any more toys tonight.'

'Well, it doesn't matter,' said the smallest goblin, in his high voice. 'We've got a whole box of toys, haven't we? By the weight of it there will be enough for all of us! Come on, let's go home.'

So they all crowded into their aeroplane and flew to their dark little cave in the green mountains. They ran the aeroplane into its shed, opened their cave-door and hopped inside, pulling the box with them. My, it certainly was heavy for those small goblins to pull!

They shut the door. They lit three candles and looked at the box.

'It's got a catch here,' said the biggest goblin. 'If two of us push hard, we can get it out of the loop it is in. Oh, I wonder if there's a doll inside? If there is, I shall have it!'

'And I shall have an engine if there is one there!' said another.

'And I shall have a humming-top!' said a third.

'And I shall have a book,' said the smallest.

'Come and help me to undo the box,' said the biggest one. 'It's very stiff, this catch.'

Two of them pushed at the catch – and suddenly it slipped back. The lid of the box flew open and out shot an enormous jack-in-the-box, much bigger than the goblins themselves, jerking about on his long spring in a very curious manner.

'Eee-eee-eee!' said the jack-in-the-box, nodding his

grinning head at the frightened goblins. 'Eee-eee-eee!'

'Ooo-ooo-ooo!' squealed the goblins, tumbling over one another, trying to get away. 'What is it? What is it?'

'Eee-eee-eee!' said the jack-in-the-box, nodding and grinning in delight. 'I'm glad you are frightened of me! Children are never frightened of jack-in-the-boxes nowadays! But I'm pleased to scare nasty little robbers like you! Eee-eee-eee!'

The goblins tore out of their cave as fast as they could. The jack-in-the-box laughed till he cried. A rabbit who was passing by heard him and looked into the cave.

'Good gracious!' said the rabbit. 'What are you?'

'A jack-in-the-box, quite harmless!' said the jack. And he told the rabbit all about how the goblins had cut a hole in Santa's sack, and made his box tumble out. He told the rabbit too how frightened they had been when he jumped out at them!

'It serves them right!' said the rabbit, grinning.

'Those goblins are a perfect nuisance! They steal and they tell stories and they scare all the little mice and hedgehogs they meet. It's a good thing someone has come along to scare them!'

'What am I going to do?' said the jack-in-the-box. 'I should really live in a house and amuse the children. But now I shall have no home and amuse no one.'

'Well, I have eight small bunnies who would love to have you,' said the rabbit. 'Come and live with us. You don't need anything to eat, do you? We will look after you and you shall jump in and out as much as you like.'

'Oh, thank you very much,' said the jack-in-the-box, delighted. 'Push me down into my box, please, rabbit; shut the lid, and fasten the catch. Then you can easily carry me down your burrow.'

So off to the rabbit's home went the merry jack-in-the-box, and dear me, how he made the young rabbits laugh when he popped in and out at them, shouting 'Eee-eee-eee!' in his funny high voice!

And do you know what the mother rabbit does sometimes, when the green goblins have been very bad? She takes the jack-in-the-box and hides him under a bush or by a big toadstool – and when those goblins come running by, the jack-in-the-box jumps out at them with a rush!

'Eee-eee-eee!' he cries, and nods about on his long, springy neck. And those goblins squeal in fright and go tumbling over and over on the grass, trying to get away. One day they'll pack up and leave their cave, and then everyone on the hill will be very pleased. Good old Jack-in-the-box!

The Christmas Tree

A Family Christmas
Part Five:

The Christmas Tree

THE CHILDREN did not forget that the Christmas tree was to be decorated the next day. This was a job they all loved. The tree always looked so pretty when it was dressed in ornaments and candles, and had the fairy doll at the top under the silver star.

'I think it's the prettiest tree in the world when the candles are lighted from top to bottom, and shine and glow,' said Susan. 'I like them so much better than the electric lights most people have. The candles seem alive somehow.'

'Where are the ornaments?' said Peter. 'I'll get them.'

'Up in a box in the loft,' said Mother. 'Now, be

careful how you go up and down that steep ladder, Peter. We don't want you with a broken leg for Christmas.'

'I'll be all right!' said Peter, and sped up to the loft. He liked the loft. It was dim and dusty and smelt old. He picked his way between trunks and boxes, and then saw the big cardboard box in which the Christmas things were stored from year to year. He lifted up the lid.

'Yes – there are the glass ornaments – and there's the fairy doll, as pink and pretty as ever – and there's the silver star, still as bright – and oh, what a lovely lot of little coloured candles and candle-clips!' said Peter.

He took the box carefully down the ladder, then down the stairs and into the hall, where the others were bringing in the Christmas tree.

'Oh, what a lovely big one!' cried Peter, in excitement. 'It's bigger than last year's, I'm sure it is. Isn't it a beauty?'

It really was. It was in the wooden tub that was used year after year. The children would soon wrap red crinkled paper round it to make it bright. They put the tree in its place, and it towered up high, taller than any of the children.

'Now we'll dress you,' cried Ann, dancing round. 'You are just an ordinary tree now, green and rather dull, with funny leaves that prick. But soon you will be a fairy tree, a magic tree, the prettiest tree in the world!'

'Hark at Ann,' said Benny. 'Come on, Ann, stop dancing about and get to work. Look, you can hang some of this silver tin foil in thin strips all over the tree – that will make it look as if it is covered with little icicles. And after that you can put bits of cotton-wool on it here and there so that it looks as if snow has fallen on the branches.'

'Don't put the cotton-wool on till I've clipped on the candles,' said Susan, busy sorting out the clips. 'You mustn't put the cotton-wool near the candles in case it catches fire.'

'I'll hang on the ornaments,' said Benny. 'I can reach nice and high. Oh – here's the red bell that looked so pretty last year – and the green ball – and here's the silver bird with a long tail, look. Hardly anything has been broken.'

'It's a well-shaped tree,' said Mother, coming up. 'It will look lovely when it's finished.'

'It's a fir-tree, isn't it?' asked Susan, busy clipping on the coloured candle-sticks, ready for the candles.

'Yes – the Christmas tree is always the same kind of tree,' said Mother. 'It's a spruce fir. You can tell a spruce because it has a spike at the top, sticking straight up to the sky.'

'Yes – very useful to tie a fairy doll to,' said Susan, looking at the straight spike at the top of their Christmas tree. 'Mother, who thought of the first Christmas tree? It's such a good idea.'

'It is, isn't it,' said Mother, cutting some coloured string into small pieces, so that she might tie small presents on the tree. 'Well, I don't exactly know who thought of the first Christmas tree, as *we* know it – but there is rather a nice old story about it.'

'Tell us, please!' said Ann, who loved a story of any kind.

'Well,' said Mother, 'one stormy Christmas Eve, long long ago, a forester and his family were sitting together round a big fire. Outside, the wind blew, and the snow made the forest white.

'Suddenly there came a knock at the door. The family looked up, startled. "Who can be in the forest at this time of the night?" said the forester, in surprise, and got up to open the door.

'Outside stood a little child, shivering with cold, tired out and hungry. The forester picked him up in amazement, and brought him into the warm room.

'"See," he said, "it is a little child. Who can he be?"

'"He must remain here for the night," said his wife, feeling the child's ice-cold hands. "We will give him hot milk to drink, and a bed to sleep in."

'"He can have my bed," said Hans, the forester's son. "I can sleep on the floor tonight. Let us put the child into my warm bed."

'So the hungry, cold child was fed and warmed, and put into Hans' bed for the night. Then the family went to sleep, Hans on the floor beside the fire.

'In the morning the forester awoke, and heard an astonishing sound. It seemed to him as if a whole choir of voices was singing. He awoke his wife, and she too heard the sweet singing.

'"It is like the singing of angels," whispered the forester. Then they looked at the child they had sheltered for the night, and saw that his face was dazzling bright. He was the Christ-Child Himself!

'In awe and wonder, the forester and his family watched the holy child. He went to the fir tree, and broke off a branch. He planted the branch firmly in the ground.

'"See," he said, "you were kind to me, and you gave me gifts of warmth and food and shelter. Now here is my gift to you – a tree that at Christmas time shall bear its fruit, so that you may always have abundance."

'And so, at Christmas time, the Christmas tree shines out in beauty, and bears gifts of many kinds.'

Mother stopped and looked round. The children were all listening, and for the moment had forgotten their task of decorating the tree.

'That was a nice story,' said Ann. 'I wish the Christ-Child had come to me. I would have given up my bed to him, and he could have had my toys as well.'

'Does the Christmas tree have real fruits?' asked Peter, trying to remember. 'This one hasn't any – only just its many branches of prickly leaves.'

'Oh, you must have seen the cones on the spruce firs,' said Susan. 'Surely you have! You know what fir cones are, silly!'

'Of course!' said Peter, remembering. 'Yes – they hang down from the branches, don't they?'

'The cones of the spruce fir do, but not the cones of the silver fir,' said Benny, who was rather good at trees. 'They sit upright. You can always tell the spruce from the silver fir by its top, too – the spruce has a sharp spear-like point but the silver fir has a bush top.'

'Oh, that's easy to remember,' said Ann. 'Why hasn't our Christmas tree any cones on it, Benny? I wish it had. I would paint them silver and make them look lovely!'

'Well, it's only a baby tree,' said Benny. 'It hasn't borne cones yet. If we plant it in the garden and let it grow year by year, it will grow cones, of course. Let's do that. It has good roots, and should be all right if we plant it out.'

'Then we can have the same tree year after year!' said Ann. 'I should like that.'

'I like its prickly needle-like leaves,' said Peter. 'See, Ann – they look as if someone had combed them neatly down the middle of the branch, and made a parting – just like you do to your hair!'

The others laughed. Peter was right – the little boughs did look as if someone had made a parting down the middle of the close-set needle-leaves.

'The fir tree isn't only useful as a Christmas tree,' said Mother, 'its straight trunk is used for lots of things that need to be quite straight. Perhaps you can think of some.'

'Masts of ships!' said Benny at once.

'Telegraph posts!' said Susan.

'You've said what I was going to say,' said Ann. 'Are they right, Mummy?'

'Quite right. The fir tree gives its trunk for both those things,' said Mother. 'People say that its name "fir" should really be "fire". It should be called the fire tree, not the fir tree, because once upon a time its gummy, resinous branches used to be broken off, lighted, and used as flaring torches.'

'Have you noticed that the fir tree's roots are very shallow?' said Benny, fixing a shining yellow ornament to a bough. 'They stand out above the ground in the wood. I should think the firs would easily fall in a strong storm.'

'Oh, they do,' said Mother. 'And sometimes, if one fir falls, it knocks down the next, and that one falls and knocks down a third tree, and so they may go on, all through the forest, making quite a path of fallen trees.'

'Like a row of dominoes each knocking down the next,' said Ann, remembering how she often stood up her dominoes in a row, and then touched the first one, which caused the whole row to fall, one after the other.

'I'm going to put the star on the top of the tree now,' said Benny, fetching a chair. 'Mum, I suppose we put a star at the top to represent the Star of Bethlehem, don't we?'

'Yes,' said Mother. 'The Christmas tree should always have the Star of Bethlehem shining at the top.'

'Have we had the custom of decorating the Christmas tree for hundreds and hundreds of years, just as we have had for the holly and mistletoe?' said Ann.

'Oh dear me no!' said Mother. 'It's not much more

than a hundred and fifty or so years ago that the first Christmas tree was set up in England. It was first known in Germany, then spread to other countries, and at length came to England. It is the kind of simple and beautiful idea that spreads into all lands. Who first thought of it we don't really know, nor quite how long ago. The idea itself may be old, but our English custom is certainly not older than the last century. Prince Albert, the husband of Queen Victoria, set up a Christmas tree at Windsor in 1841 – and after that the tree was used in England.'

'It must be nice to begin a custom like this,' said Ann. 'I wish I could begin one of my own.'

'Isn't the tree beginning to look lovely?' said Susan, stepping back a little to see it. 'How the ornaments shine – and the tinfoil strips gleam – and the star glitters. I'm longing for the time when the candles will all be lighted.'

It took the children all the morning to decorate the tree properly, but they loved every minute of it. By the time it was finished there was not a bough without a candle, present or ornament, and the frosted cotton-wool and strips of tinfoil gave the tree a glitter and shine that made it very beautiful.

The star shone at the top, and under it stood the fairy doll, a silver crown on her head, silver wings behind her and a silver wand in her hand. Little presents for every member of the household hung here and there, wrapped in coloured paper.

'They are *proper* presents,' said Mother, 'not useful gifts, which should never be put on a Christmas tree according to old beliefs – but beautiful little gifts which will bring joy and pleasure to everyone.'

'How lovely,' said Ann, dancing round. 'Now the tree is beautiful. Mummy, I wouldn't be surprised if all the other trees in the garden came close to the window and looked in when we light our Christmas tree!'

'You do say funny things,' said Benny laughing, but they all thought secretly that it was rather a quaint idea of Ann's, and could quite imagine the hollies and the yews, the birches and the oaks pressing themselves against the window to see the beauty of the lighted Christmas tree.

'It's finished, it's finished!' said Ann. 'Now it only has to wait in patience to be lighted from top to toe!'

'I'm so hungry,' said Peter. 'I say – what are we going to do after lunch?'

'I'm going to do some more Christmas cards,' said Susan, 'and wrap up some presents. And I am making some crackers too – though I haven't any "cracks" to put into them to go pop when they are pulled. But I know how to make lovely crackers. We did some at school this term.'

'Well – you will be very busy,' said Mother. 'I will come and help you all. We will have a nice Christmassy afternoon.'

The Tiny
Christmas Tree

The Tiny Christmas Tree

THERE WAS once a very small Christmas tree. It lived in the woods among all the other Christmas trees that were grown for Christmas-time.

You should have seen those Christmas trees. They were all planted in straight rows, and they were fine sturdy trees.

There were rows of trees about three feet high, just big enough for a small nursery. Then there were rows of bigger trees, whose branches could take quite a lot of toys and ornaments. Then there were bigger trees still for parties – the kind of Christmas trees that almost touch the ceiling of the drawing-room, and look simply wonderful when they have candles lighted.

And largest of all were the trees that were sold for school-parties – the sort that tower right up high, and hold hundreds of presents, and sparkle like magic. Oh, you would have loved to see all the green Christmas trees growing in rows, waiting for someone to come and buy them for Christmas!

'I shall be sold this Christmas, I am sure,' said one tree, whispering to its neighbour. 'I am sturdy and straight and strong. I am a fine tree. They will dress me in silvery frost and glittering ornaments and shining candles, and they will hang me with marvellous toys.'

'I shall be sold too,' said a tree in the next row. 'I am sure I shall have a fairy-doll put right at the top. I have a straight little spike there that a doll could be tied to. How marvellous I shall look!'

'And how the children will clap their hands and shout for joy when they see *me*,' said the biggest tree of all. 'My goodness – I shall look grand, I can tell you. I've been sold already. Somebody bought me yesterday. Did you see her coming round and looking at all the trees? She said to the tree-grower, "I will have that tree for Christmas. Mark it for me, please. It is a magnificent tree and will stand nicely in my great hall when I give a Christmas party to all the children in the village." Think of that! I shall be so proud.'

Now the very small Christmas tree felt sad. Nobody had ever thought of buying it. It really was so very small. The trees in the row it grew in were all much bigger. It could not understand why it had not grown.

'I wonder if I shall ever be bought,' said the little fir tree sadly. 'I don't think I shall ever be much use. I have hardly grown since I was two years old. All the others have put out new spikes and branches at the top, and have grown higher and higher. But I stay small all the time.'

The other trees teased the small Christmas tree.

'Why don't you grow?' they said. 'You are a little dwarf tree, a toy tree, a tree that should stand in a child's garden, because you are so small. Funny little tree!'

When Christmas week came, many people walked among the rows of Christmas trees, choosing their trees for the parties. All the trees that were in the tiny tree's row were bought, and they were full of glee.

'We shall be dug up this week, put into pots, and travel away to our great adventure!' they cried. 'Oh, how grand we shall be! How we shall love all the children who dance round us!'

Only the tiny tree was sad. Nobody had bought it. Some of the people had laughed at it.

'What a funny little tree!' they said. 'Why do you keep it? Why don't you dig it up and throw it away?'

That made the little tree shiver with fright. It was very unhappy when the man came to dig up all its friends and put them into fine red pots.

'Goodbye, goodbye,' the little tree said to each one.

'Have a good time. Be beautiful and grand, and give joy to hundreds of children. Goodbye!'

There were very few trees left when the day before Christmas came. There were none near the little fir tree at all. The cold wind blew all round him and he trembled in the frost. He was sad and lonely.

Then a little boy and girl came running towards the trees. They stopped beside the tiny tree.

'This one would do beautifully,' said the little girl.

'It's just about the right size,' said the boy. 'Let's ask if we may have it.'

So they went to the tree-grower and he came out with them. He looked at the tiny tree.

'You can have it for nothing,' he said. 'It's no use to me, because it won't grow. I was going to dig it up and throw it away. Something is the matter with it.'

'Well, we shall love to have it,' said the boy, and he and the girl dug up the tiny tree. They fetched a small pot for it, put it into the boy's barrow, and wheeled it away to a house down the road.

The fir tree was most excited. 'What is going to happen to me?' it wondered. 'Surely, surely, I can't be going to be a real dressed-up Christmas tree after all?'

Then it caught sight of a big tree it knew! It was a fir tree out of the row that had been next to the tiny tree. 'Hallo!' said the big tree, in surprise. It was standing in the yard in a fine big pot. 'Hallo! Fancy seeing *you*! What have you come here for?'

'Well, I was just hoping I might be a real Christmas tree after all,' said the small tree.

'Well, you won't,' said the big tree. 'I'm here to be dressed up for the Christmas parties. The children told me so. Goodness knows what they want *you* for!'

The little tree was sad. It stood in the yard beside the big tree and wondered why it had been brought there.

Soon the children came out. They began to hang silver threads of frost on the branches of the little tree. They hung six ornaments on it too – a red one, a green one, a yellow one, and three blue ones. They did look lovely. The little tree felt very grand.

'Well, I *must* be going to be a Christmas tree!' it said to itself. 'I wonder if the children will hang toys on me next.'

But they didn't. They hung some rather strange things! They took a coconut and broke it into bits. They made holes in the middle of the bits and threaded them with string. Then they tied the bits of coconut to the branches, just as if they were toys! The little tree was really astonished.

Then the children brought out some bits of bacon-rind and they hung those on the tree, too. They brought out a bone and tied that to one of the strongest branches! The tree was more and more surprised.

'Are they making fun of me?' he wondered, when he heard the big tree laughing at him. 'I don't understand this at all!'

Then the children tied crusts of bread and biscuits on to the tree, and then three fine sprays of millet-seeds that the birds love so much.

'There! It's finished!' said the boy. 'Now help me to carry it to the bird-table, Janet. Doesn't it look lovely?'

The bird-table was in the front garden. The children put the little tree right in the middle of it and then stepped back to look at it.

'Isn't our birds' Christmas tree beautiful?' they cried. 'Mummy, come and look! We were lucky to get this little tiny tree. It's just the right size for the bird-table! We've put everything on it that the birds like, and we have made it pretty with frosty threads and shining ornaments! It looks just as lovely as the big tree will look!'

The tiny tree shook with pride. So it was a real Christmas tree after all! A birds' Christmas tree! Could anything be nicer? The little fir tree loved the birds that hopped in the trees and sang – now it was going to give them pleasure and feed them all day long. It was so happy that it wished it could sing like a blackbird.

The birds soon came to it. The tits pecked at

the coconut. The starlings took the fat. The chaffinches pecked the sprays of millet. The sparrows and the robins loved the biscuits. There was something for everybody.

All day long the little fir tree felt the tiny cold feet of the birds in its branches. There is nothing that a tree loves more than that, except the wind that blows through it. The passers-by stopped to look at the tree on the bird-table, and they loved it.

'Look!' they said. 'Look! A birds' Christmas tree! Isn't that a good idea? Let's do one ourselves next winter! How lovely it looks with all the birds on it!'

When Christmas was over, the tiny tree was not thrown away. Oh no! The children planted it out in the garden carefully.

'We'll dig you up next winter again,' they said. 'Grow a little bit, and we can hang more things on you. And when you are too big for a birds' Christmas tree, we'll have you for our own Christmas tree and put candles on you and toys. You are such a dear little tree!'

The tree is very happy now. It grows next to a big lilac and some gooseberry bushes, and it tells them all about how it was a birds' Christmas tree last Christmas.

I wonder if you'd like to have a little tree like that, too, and put it out for the birds? Buy a little tiny one, if you can, and dress it up for the birds. You'll have such a lot of fun watching the sparrows, the robins, the chaffinches, and the tits pecking at the things you have hung on their own special tree!

A Christmassy
Afternoon

A Family Christmas
Part Six:

A Christmassy Afternoon

IT WAS snowing when the children settled down that afternoon to finish off their Christmas preparations. The next day was Christmas Eve – a most exciting day, when presents were labelled and hidden away for Christmas morning, and when stockings were hung up at night.

'What lovely cards you do,' said Ann, looking over Susan's shoulder at the card she was painting very neatly. 'I do like that robin – and the snow on the roofs of the houses is very real.'

'It's the writing that spoils my cards,' said Susan. 'I can't seem to write nearly as neatly as Benny.'

Benny's cards were certainly beautifully done. His Christmas messages inside were written in gold ink, the capitals outlined in black or red.

Ann and Peter had finished their cards and posted them. They felt quite glad that the elder children hadn't seen them, because they were not nearly so beautiful as theirs.

The mantelpiece was full of cards that had come for the family. They were so pretty, all sizes and shapes and colours. Some were very plain and neat, others were merry and bright.

The children loved the cards. They looked at each one carefully, and always read the little messages inside. They thought cards at Christmas were a very good idea.

Mother was sitting by the fire, doing some mending. The children liked having her there. They could ask her how to spell words, and could show her their cards as they finished them.

'Who first thought of Christmas cards?' said Susan,

drawing a very fat and cheerful-looking robin. 'Is it a very old custom, Mother, like the others we've heard about?'

'No, it isn't,' said Mother. 'I do know a little about Christmas cards, because your great grandfather's firm was one of the first to print them. But the first cards were not printed, they were written.'

'How do you mean?' asked Benny.

'Well, at the beginning of the last century, schoolboys had to write compositions and decorate the sheets of paper on which they wrote them, in order to show their parents how they had improved in their writing,' said Mother. 'They took these Christmas compositions home with them, and presented them to their parents, who, of course, were proud of them, and stood them up on the mantelpiece for everyone to see.'

'Oh – like you stand up my drawings that I bring home from school!' said Ann.

'Yes,' said Mother. 'Well, for some years these Christmas papers were done by schoolboys, and then a few grown-ups thought it would be a good idea if they too sent Christmas messages, hand-written on decorated paper, to their friends. So they did, and these private Christmas greetings became quite popular.'

'And so, I suppose, people then began to have them printed?' said Benny, looking up.

'Yes,' said his mother. 'It became the fashion to send a printed card with a Christmas greeting on it to friends – it was a simple and kindly way of remembering them at Christmas time. At first, of course, the cards were very very simple – just a sprig of holly or mistletoe, or a little fat robin like the one on Susan's cards.'

'Then did they get like the ones we have now, Mother?' said Ann, looking at the brilliant array on the mantelpiece. 'Really, some of the cards sent aren't a bit Christmassy, just pretty pictures that could be sent at any time of the year.'

'Well, there were all kinds of fashions in cards,'

said Mother. 'Wait, I've got a few old ones that your great-grandfather gave me. Fetch me the box on the top of the bookcase in my room, Benny.'

Benny fetched it and Mother opened it. In it were some old Christmas cards. Some of the oldest were, as Mother had said, quite simple and plain – but then came glittering ones, frosted all over. Ann liked those.

'These are nice,' she said. 'See how they shine. The frost must be stuck on. It rubs off a bit when I scratch it with my nail. Look, my finger is shining with it. I like these frosted cards, Mother.'

'Your great-grandfather used to send these to his friends,' said Mother. 'And now look at these silk-fringed ones. We don't see these nowadays. Great-grandfather had them sent to him. I suppose you like these too, Ann?'

Ann did, though Susan thought they were too elaborate. She liked something simpler.

'Nowadays if we want a really nice card we choose

a beautiful reproduction of the Nativity, or some fine religious picture – or we look for some really artistic card,' said their Mother. 'We do not go in for show.'

'I like the cards *I* get,' said Ann, looking at hers that stood beside the clock. 'There's one that has a bear popping out with a Christmas message when you open it, Mummy. And here's one I like – see when it's opened, a Christmas tree stands up, with presents on! And here's one with a little window – when you open it, you see Santa Claus peeping out!'

'Yes – children's cards are amusing and clever nowadays,' said Mother, shutting up her box of old Christmas cards, with their glittering frost and silky fringes. 'Each generation has its own ideas, its likes and dislikes.'

'It's interesting to know that even a little thing like a Christmas card has its own history,' said Benny, finishing off a card with a flourish. 'Who did the very first card, I wonder?'

'I'm going to make my crackers now,' said Susan, getting out some red, yellow and green crinkled paper. 'Like to help me, Ann? Look, it's quite easy. I use this white paper for the lining – and put my little present inside – then I cut the crinkled paper to the right size – and roll it . . .'

'And nip it at the two ends – and tie the nips with that coloured tinsel thread,' said Ann. 'And then glue a picture on the front. I didn't think it would be as easy as that to make crackers.'

'Mummy, do you know the story of the Christmas cracker?' said Benny, beginning another card.

'No, I don't,' said Mother. 'I only know they are about a hundred and fifty years old. When my mother was a child they used to be called "bon-bons," and they had sweets inside.'

'I suppose they are called "crackers" because they go off with a crack when we pull them,' said Susan, sticking a scrap on to the first cracker she had made.

'Where are you going, Mummy?' asked Ann, seeing her mother get up.

'Just to take the Christmas pudding off the stove,' said Mother. 'I left it boiling. It will be nice and black for Christmas Day now.'

Their mother came back after a while, and the children had more questions ready for her.

'Did we always have a feast at Christmas time, for hundreds and hundreds of years?'

'Why do we have a turkey?'

'Why aren't there any plums in the plum pudding?'

'Is there any old reason for hiding things in the pudding?'

'How did mince-pies begin?'

'My goodness me, I'm not an encyclopedia!' said Mother. 'Ah – listen – that's Daddy home early, I'm sure. You can pick *his* brains a little now, and give me a rest.'

So, when Daddy came in to find his family, he was greeted by another list of Christmas questions.

'Why, why, why? When? How?'

'One question at a time!' he said. 'Yes, Christmas feasting is very old – but I daresay you children would have enjoyed it most in Queen Elizabeth's time. They really did know how to feast in those days. Even you, Peter, would have had more than enough to eat!'

Everyone laughed. Peter's enormous appetite was always a joke.

'Did they have the boar's head carried in, in those days?' asked Benny.

'The boar's head? Whatever's that?' said Ann, in surprise. 'What's a boar?'

'A pig,' said Daddy. 'Yes, at Christmas time in the old days, servants carried in a great silver dish, wreathed with bay leaves, on which was a roasted boar's head. In the boar's mouth was put an apple or a lemon, and its ears were decorated with sprigs of rosemary. Carols were sung as it was brought in – it was a great sight!'

'I wish I could see it,' said Peter, his eyes shining.

'Well, if you were at Queen's College, Oxford, you could, because the old custom is still followed there,' said his father.

'Do they sing a carol when the boar's head is brought in?' asked Peter.

'Yes – it is in Latin – and the words mean something like this,' said Daddy:

> *'The Boar's head in hand bear I*
> *Bedecked with bays and rosemary;*
> *And I pray you, my masters, be merry,*
> *I bear the Boar's head,*
> *Rendering praise to the Lord.'*

'Did they bring in turkeys too, in the old days with the boar's head?' asked Ann. 'We've got a most enormous turkey hanging in the larder. I've seen it.'

'No, they didn't bring in turkeys,' said Daddy. 'That's quite a new custom, which we get from America. The goose used to be the bird we most often had at Christmas time in England. But beef, the "Roast Beef of Old England" has always been our greatest Christmas dish. We have always enjoyed our sirloin of beef – or our baron of beef which is two sirloins joined together.'

'Why is it called sirloin?' wondered Peter. 'We don't say sirloin of lamb, do we?'

'Well, you see, they say Charles II thought so much of loin of beef as a dish that he actually knighted it,' said Daddy, with a laugh. 'You can see him doing it, can't you – striking it with his sword, and saying "Rise, Sir Loin!"'

'Oh, is that really how the sirloin got its name?' said Peter, amused. 'Fancy knighting food you like. I've a good mind to knight chocolate ice-cream.'

'The Queen always has a baron of beef served on her table at Christmas time I've heard,' said Mother. 'Dick, do you know anything about Christmas pudding? The children keep asking why it's called plum pudding when it has no plums in it. I suppose the old name contains its history?'

'Yes, it does,' said Daddy. 'In the old days the

people at Christmas time ate a dish called frumenty, which was really stewed wheat grains. This gradually became plum porridge, and then plum pudding. It was then made of beef or mutton broth thickened with brown bread, raisins, currants, prunes, spices and gingerbread.'

'Prunes are really plums, aren't they?' said Susan. 'Is that why the pudding was called plum pudding?'

'Well, people in those days used to call even raisins and currants "plums",' said Daddy. 'Now, of course, we don't even put prunes, or plums, into the pudding, so we really oughtn't to call it plum pudding at all. Christmas pudding is a much better name.'

'We don't put broth into the pudding either!' said Mother, 'and we do put into it a great many things that the old people never thought of – ground-up nuts, for instance – and . . .'

'And silver thimbles and money and little horse-shoes for luck,' said Ann.

'Well, I don't know how *that* habit began,' said

Daddy. 'I've never heard. It was probably started just for a joke, and was such fun that it became popular!'

'What about mince-pies?' said Peter. 'We're going to have some, aren't we, Mum?'

'Of course!' said his mother. 'We couldn't have Christmas without mince pies!'

'Well, you wouldn't have known the mince pies of olden days,' said Daddy. 'They were pies *really* filled with minced meat, as their name tells you. The first minced pies were filled with things like chopped-up hare, pheasant, capon, partridge and so on; then, later on, sweeter things were put into the pies, such as raisins, oranges, sugar and spices – but they were still called mince pies, though there was no longer any minced meat in them.'

'Nowadays mince pies are very sweet to the taste,' said Mother. 'They are a sweet-course, not a meat-course. You must all remember to eat your pies in silence, so that you may have happiness for a month next year, each time you eat a mince pie!'

'Another old custom,' said Susan. 'I like that one. I don't know what Peter did last year, about his "happy months," Mother, because he ate fourteen mince pies, and there are only twelve months in a year.'

'Oh, the thirteenth and fourteenth pies ran into next year!' said Peter, grinning. 'I could do with a mince pie this minute!'

'Well, how funny – because we're having them for tea!' said Mummy. Sure enough, at tea time on a dish were piled the first mince pies, one for everybody. How Peter's eyes gleamed.

'Good!' he said. 'Thank you, Mum. Just what I wanted. Now I'll be able to wish a happy month next year. That will take me to March!'

Susan put away her crackers. Benny put away his cards. They were all ready for tea. It was nice sitting there in the living room with the big fire glowing, and the holly round the walls, its berries shining red.

'Tomorrow is Christmas Eve!' said Susan. 'And we will bring in the old Yule log!'

What Happened
on Christmas Eve

'What Happened on Christmas Eve

'NOW – ARE we all ready?' asked Santa Claus, standing by his reindeer sleigh. 'Sack in? All the toys in it that I asked for – especially those new aeroplanes for the boys? Have the reindeer had a good feed?'

'Yes, sir,' said his little servant. 'Look at them stamping their feet and tossing their antlers in the air! They are longing to go. Goodbye, sir; I hope you have a good journey. You will find you have plenty of toys in the sack, and you know the spell to use if you want some more.'

'Right,' said Santa Claus and stepped into his sleigh. 'Brrrrrr! It's a cold and frosty night. Pull the rug closely round my feet, please.'

He was well tucked-in. He took the reins and clicked to the four impatient reindeer. 'Get along, then! Up into the air with you – and for goodness' sake look out for telegraph wires before you land on anyone's roof!'

Bells began to ring very loudly as the reindeer galloped over the snow and then rose smoothly in the air, their feet still galloping. Only reindeer belonging to Santa Claus could gallop through the air. They loved that. It was a wonderful feeling.

They soon left the sky over Toyland and galloped into the sky over our land. The moon sailed up and lighted everything. Santa Claus peered downwards.

'We're there! Go a bit lower, reindeer, I must just look at my notebook to see the names there.'

'Peter Jones, Sara White, Ben White, Michael Andrews . . . they all live somewhere here. Land on a roof nearby, reindeer.'

The reindeer galloped downwards. The biggest

one looked out for telegraph wires. The year before he had caught his hooves in some and had nearly upset the sleigh. He guided the others safely down to a big roof, where a large chimney stood.

Santa Claus got out and pulled his sack from the sleigh. 'Two children here,' he said. 'Sara and Ben White. Good children, too. I shall leave them some nice toys.'

He disappeared down the chimney. The reindeer waited patiently. One of them began to paw at the roof, and then stopped quickly. He remembered that he had been told never to do that. It might wake up the children of the house if they heard someone knocking on the roof!

The breath of the reindeer looked like steam in the frosty, moonlit air. They stood and stared out over the quiet town. This was a big adventure for them, and they enjoyed every minute of it.

Santa Claus popped his head out of the chimney. 'Give me a pull,' he said to the biggest reindeer.

The reindeer turned his big head and put his mouth down to Santa Claus's neck. He tugged at the back of his cloak there, and Santa Claus came up with a jerk, his sack after him.

'Thanks,' he said. 'I must have got a bit fatter. I never got stuck in that chimney before. The two children were fast asleep, reindeer. They *have* grown since last year. The girl has stopped biting her nails. I noticed that. I gave her a specially nice doll because I felt so pleased.'

'Hrrrrumph,' said the reindeer, sounding pleased too. In a minute or two they were all galloping off at top speed again, the bells jingling.

Santa Claus was very busy. He left toys here, there and everywhere. Then he came to a little village and peered downwards. 'There are two children somewhere down there,' he said. 'Let me see – what were their names? Ah, yes – Elizabeth and Jonathan. Now – where's my notebook? What shall I leave them this year?'

He turned the pages and looked down a list of names. 'Oh dear! The report I had of them this year isn't good. They've been rude to their mother – and have been lazy at school. I'm afraid I can't leave them anything. And they did seem such nice children last year. What a pity! Reindeer – go on to the next big town, please. There are a lot of children there.'

And then something happened. An aeroplane came flying by, fairly low, just as the reindeer galloped upwards into the frosty sky. There wasn't a collision because the biggest reindeer swerved at once – but the aeroplane caused such a tremendous current of air, as it passed close to the sleigh, that Santa Claus felt himself being blown off! He clutched at the side of the sleigh and just managed to hold on, though his legs were blown over the side and he had to climb back very carefully indeed.

He sat down and mopped his forehead. 'My word! What a narrow escape!' he said. 'I feel quite faint. Go slowly to the next town, reindeer. I've had a fright.'

So they went very slowly indeed, and Santa Claus lay back in his rugs and got over the shock. He didn't know that his sack of toys had been blown right out of the sleigh!

It had risen in the air when the aeroplane almost bumped into them, and had then dropped downwards. It landed with a tremendous thud on the roof of a house, burst open, and flung all the toys inside to the ground. They rolled down the roof one by one – ships, dolls, balls, teddy bears, trains and all.

Bumpity-bump! Clitter-clat! Rillobyroll! Down they went and fell all over the garden below.

The two children in the house were wide awake. They hadn't been to sleep at all. They were Elizabeth and Jonathan Frost, the two children that Santa Claus was not going to give any toys to because their school reports had been bad, and because they had been so rude to their mother that year.

They hadn't been able to go to sleep because they were unhappy. Their mother was ill in hospital – just at Christmas-time! Nothing could be worse.

'I wouldn't feel so bad about it if only we hadn't been so horrid to Mother,' said Jonathan. 'She never said a word about being ill – and we kept on being rude. Whatever came over us to be so horrid?'

'I don't know,' said Elizabeth. 'And now we've upset Daddy too, because our bad school reports came on the very day Mother went to hospital – just as if he hadn't already had too much bad luck. I feel awful. I wish we'd had good reports to cheer up poor Daddy.'

'There won't be any presents this Christmas,' said Jonathan gloomily. 'Mother away – Daddy upset. Nobody will think about us at all.'

'Well, Mrs Brown next door said it served us right to have a miserable Christmas,' said Elizabeth. 'She said she'd heard us being cheeky to Mother. And she said if we hadn't been so horrid to poor Mother, she would have bought us presents herself, but she didn't think we deserved any.'

'Well, we don't,' said Jonathan. 'We've been simply . . . I say! What's that noise? It sounds like bells!'

It *was* bells. The children listened. Then they heard another sound. 'An aeroplane!' said Elizabeth. 'Isn't it low? I wonder what those bells were.'

Suddenly there was a tremendous thud on the roof. Crash! Then came lots of other, smaller noises. *Bumpity-bump! Clitter-clat! Rilloby-roll!*

The children sat up straight and looked out of the window. In the moonlight they saw a lot of little dark things falling. Whatever was happening?

'What is it?' said Jonathan, scared. 'Something fell on the roof. Do you think it was something the aeroplane dropped? Shall we go and look?'

'Yes,' said Elizabeth, scrambling out of bed. She dragged on her thick robe and put on warm slippers. 'Quick! Come and see.'

They went down the stairs and opened the back door. Scattered all over the garden were many little dark things. Elizabeth picked up the first one and looked at it in the moonlight.

'Jonathan! It's a doll! The prettiest one I ever saw in my life. Do look!'

But Jonathan was picking up a train and a big ship with magnificent sails and three teddy-bears in a row together! Elizabeth began to pick up things, too. Another doll, two fat toy pandas, a doll's house with its chimney off, a musical box. Really there seemed to be no end to the toys in their garden that night!

The children piled them all together and went through them again. What a wonderful collection! Elizabeth nursed each of the dolls, and Jonathan wound up the train to see if the clockwork was still all right.

'*Where* did they come from? Did that aeroplane really drop them?' said Elizabeth.

'No, I don't think so,' said Jonathan. 'You know, Elizabeth, I think Santa Claus must have galloped over here and he's dropped his sack of toys. Look up on the roof. That looks like a big, burst-open sack there, doesn't it?'

It did. The children stared at it. 'Well – I suppose we can't keep any of these lovely things then,' said Elizabeth with a sigh. 'I do love this baby doll so much. What shall we do with everything?'

'I expect when Santa Claus misses his sack, he will come back and look for it,' said Jonathan. 'We had better put everything into one of our own sacks – there are plenty in the shed. We will leave it standing in the garden for him to see. He will easily spot it in the moonlight.'

'I wish we could keep just one thing each,' said Elizabeth.

'Well, we can't,' said Jonathan. 'For one thing the toys aren't ours. And for another thing you know jolly well we don't deserve anything.'

They found a big sack and put everything into it. Just as they were tying up the neck, they heard the sound of bells again – and there, up in the bright moonlit sky, they saw the reindeer sleigh, and Santa Claus leaning over, looking downwards. He saw the children, of course, and down he came, the reindeer landing softly in the garden snow.

'Your sack fell on our roof!' said Jonathan, running up to help him out of the sleigh. 'We've collected all the toys, sir, and put them into another sack. Here they are!'

'What good, honest children!' beamed Santa Claus, taking the big sack from them. 'I'm sure I must have your names down on my list. I'll let you *choose* your Christmas toys, for being such a help. Let me see, what *are* your names?'

'Elizabeth and Jonathan, Santa Claus,' said Elizabeth.

Santa Claus at once looked solemn. 'Oh! I'm sorry – your names are *not* down on my list for presents this year. Bad work at school – and rudeness to your mother. What a pity!'

The children went red. 'Yes,' said Jonathan. 'It's

more than a pity, Santa Claus. Our mother's ill and in hospital, and we can't forgive ourselves for making her unhappy. And our father has just had our bad reports when he's feeling miserable about Mother. I can tell you we're going to turn over a new leaf next year!'

'Yes, we're both going to be top of our forms, and we're going to make such a fuss of Mother when she comes home that she will be happier than she's ever been before!' said Elizabeth. 'We didn't expect any presents from you this year. We haven't even hung our stockings up.'

'Well – it's good to see children who are not ashamed to own up when they've done wrong,' said Santa Claus. 'I think I'd better leave you two little things, just as a reward for picking up all my toys for me.'

'We'd rather you left Mother something at the hospital,' said Jonathan. 'She broke her watch the day before she was ill. Could you leave her a new one, do you think?'

'Oh yes!' said Santa Claus. 'I'll do that. Goodbye and thank you – and just see that I have your names down on my list for *next* Christmas!'

He drove off into the air with a jingling of bells, and the children went to bed, feeling sleepy. They were fast asleep in two minutes.

In the morning, what a surprise! Standing at the end of Elizabeth's bed was the big baby doll she had picked up the night before – and at the end of Jonathan's was the toy train!

'He came back! Oh, he's the kindest old fellow in the world!' cried Elizabeth. 'Jonathan, I do hope he remembered Mother's watch.'

He did, of course. She was even more surprised than the children to find such a lovely present by her bedside – and one that nobody knew anything about at all!

'Well, that was an adventure that did a lot of good!' said Santa Claus, as he galloped back to Toyland that night. 'It's nice to meet children who know how to turn over a new leaf. What a surprise they'll get on Christmas morning! I wonder if their names will be down on my list for next Christmas.'

Of course they will, Santa Claus! We can all tell you that for certain!

Bringing in the Yule Log

A Family Christmas
Part Seven:

Bringing in the Yule Log

THE SNOW was falling again when the children looked out of the window after breakfast. It had fallen in the night too, and the ground was white.

'The snow is thick enough for us to use sledges,' said Benny, pleased. 'That will be an easy way to bring in the big Yule log, Mum. Has Daddy cut it down for us?'

'Yes,' said Mother. 'It is at the top of the garden. You can go and see it, but you had better wait till Daddy comes home to bring it in. Then he can help to lift it on the big fire in the living room. It is too heavy for you.'

'I don't know any family but ours that brings in the Yule log,' said Susan, as they went up the garden to see the great log waiting for them.

'Well, think of our big old fireplace in the living room!' said Benny. 'You can only bring in a proper Yule log if you have an open fireplace where you can have a real fire. Not many people have those these days.'

'Oh, yes, of course,' said Susan. 'I forgot that most people don't have real fires now. I'm glad we live in the country in an old house so we can bring in a proper Yule log and burn it on Christmas Eve.'

'Look – there it is,' said Ann, dancing up to it. 'What a beauty! It will just go into our hearth nicely – but Mummy will have to have a very big fire ready to burn it!'

It really was a fine big log. John, their next-door neighbour was looking over the fence, and he smiled when he saw the children.

'There's a wonderful log for you,' he said. 'And I've

got one for myself too, over there, look!'

He pointed to another log, not so long as theirs, but very big and broad.

'Oh, have you got a big enough fire-place in your old cottage?' asked Ann.

'Yes, I have,' said John. 'They built big chimneys in the days when my cottage was put up, and my kitchen hearth is half the kitchen. My, it's a warm place when we've got a log like that burning.'

'We could put our log on our sledge and drag it over the snow when Daddy comes,' said Peter.

'How are you going to get yours home, John?'

'I'll haul it behind me on a rope,' said John. 'It'll run easy enough on the snow. My old grandad, he used to haul in a Yule log each year too, and he used to light it with a bit of the old Yule log that he'd had the year before. Somehow he managed to keep a bit of it by him, and he always said that he lighted one Yule log from another, down the years.'

'Oh, I hadn't heard of that,' said Susan, pleased.

'We'll do that too. We'll keep a bit of this log till *next* Christmas, and then light the new one from it – and then we'll keep a bit of the next one, and light the following Yule log from that – and ...'

'You needn't go on down the century,' said Benny laughing. 'We know what you mean. We'll tell Mum, and get her to save a bit.'

'Why is it called the Yule log, John?' asked Ann, walking along the log. 'I know Yule means Christmas, but why do we call it the Yule log instead of the Christmas log?'

'I don't know I'm afraid,' said John. 'All I know is that in days gone by, bringing in the Yule log was a proper ceremony – you know, singing and merry-making and all. Seems like we've got no time for things like that nowadays.'

'We do other things instead,' said Benny. 'Did your grandfather follow other old customs as well as bringing in the Yule log, John?'

'Oh yes,' said John, beginning to saw some wood

up. 'He went mumming.'

'Mumming? What's mumming?' said Peter, who had never heard the word.

'Oh, mummers got themselves all dressed up and went out singing and dancing round people's houses,' said John. 'Sometimes boys dressed up as girls, and girls as boys. I remember my grandfather saying he had to act, and do a lot of made-up fighting.'

'I should like to go out mumming,' said Benny, thinking about it. 'And I'd like to wassail too!'

'Wassail? What a funny word! How do you wassail?' said Ann, jumping off the log.

'Wassailing is just drinking people's health out of the wassail bowl,' said Benny, rather grandly. 'It's a very old custom too, like mumming. People used to go wassailing at Christmas time and New Year's Day. We don't do it now.'

'Let's go and make a snowman,' said Peter, not very interested in wassailing. 'Then we can have a snowfight.'

So they went off to play in the snow, leaving the Yule log to get white in the falling flakes. They forgot about it till their father came home to tea and wanted to know if they had seen the Yule log.

'Oh yes!' said Benny. 'It's a beauty. It was too heavy for us to bring in alone. Let's go and get it now.'

'I've got a fine fire burning in the living room hearth,' said Mother, stirring it up. 'Go and get the log now, before it is too dark, and we will put it on.'

'Then there will be a lovely fire for you to tell us the Christmas story by, and for us to sing carols round,' said Ann, rushing to get her coat.

So, with coats thrown round them, and scarves over their heads, everyone hurried up the snowy garden to where the Yule log lay, hidden under a thick covering of snow. Benny pulled his sledge behind him.

Somehow they all got the big, heavy log on to the sledge. Then, with everyone giving a hand to the ropes, the Yule log was brought triumphantly into the house. It was taken to the lounge, and rolled into the fire.

Sizzle, sizzle, sizzle, went the melting snow as the flames licked it away. Then, after a while, the log began to blaze, and soon was well alight. Everyone watched it with pleasure, especially the four children.

'Do you remember the story I told you of Balder the bright and the beautiful?' said their father, as they watched the log burn. 'Well, the old Norsemen, who believed in the gods I told you about then, used to burn a log each year to the great god Thor, who also dwelt in Asgard.'

'Why is it called Yule log?' asked Benny.

'It probably comes from the name that the old Norsemen used to give Odin, the father of the gods,' said Daddy. 'He was called "Jul-Vatter" or "Yule-Father"; Yule was a word meaning "sun" and the god Odin was supposed to be the sun himself. The old Norsemen kept a festival of the sun just about this time of year – a "Jul" or Yule festival – so I suppose the name has come down through the years, and now means Christmas-time, which we hold at the same time as the old Norsemen held their sun or Yule festival.'

The log blazed up and sparks flew off. Mother turned out the light. 'We'll sit and watch it,' she said. 'It's a pretty sight, to see a big log burning.'

They all sat down, and watched the glowing fire. Susan told her father how John had said his grandfather had gone mumming.

'That's interesting,' said her father. 'Mumming is a very old custom of the country, but I don't think it happens anymore these days.'

'Is pantomime anything to do with mumming?' said Benny, getting a little further back from the hot fire. 'They're both acting, aren't they?'

'Yes – but they are not the same thing,' said Daddy. 'Pantomime is acting in a silent show – no word should be spoken at all – that is true pantomime, and that is how pantomime began.'

'Good gracious!' said Susan, thinking of the lovely

pantomimes she had seen, 'no word spoken! Why, in the pantomimes I have seen, the actors speak and sing all the time!'

'Yes, that is true,' said Daddy. 'So they shouldn't really be called pantomimes at all. If you had seen real pantomime in the long-ago days, you would simply have seen actors, not singers, or talkers – men coming on, acting in silence to show some well-known story, which could easily be followed by the delighted audience.'

'And that was the beginning of our gorgeous pantomimes!' said Susan, surprised. 'It doesn't seem possible.'

'Well, the early pantomime underwent all kinds of changes,' said father. 'And different countries had different kinds. Gradually it altered – singing was brought in, masks were used and at one stage pantomime became the ballet, which is again quite a different thing.'

'I like the pantomime as it is *now*,' said Ann,

decidedly. 'I like all the singing and dancing and jokes, and those lovely scenes. Oh – do you remember, Susan, in *Cinderella* when the pumpkin and rats turned into a coach and horses? I did love that.'

'Yes, pantomime in our country is a very entertaining thing,' said Daddy. 'No other country has anything quite like it, with its gorgeous scenes, and its bits of fairy-tale interwoven here and there.'

'We're going after Christmas, aren't we?' said Ann, feeling excited at the very thought. 'We're going to see *Aladdin and the Wonderful Lamp*. I shall love that.'

The clock struck six. 'Well,' said Mummy, 'what about a few carols? Then I will tell you the Christmas story as usual – and then – supper and bed-time!'

The Little
Reindeer Bell

The Little
Reindeer Bell

NOW IT happened one year that Santa Claus had to put a new reindeer with the others in his sleigh, because one of his old ones had a dreadful cough.

'I'll have to have someone in place of you, Quickfoot,' said Santa Claus. 'You'd wake up all the children on Christmas Eve by coughing on the roofs of their houses. I never heard such a cough in my life. Go to your stable and keep warm.'

'Sir, I think young Quick-as-the-Wind would do well,' said the stable-man. 'He's a young reindeer, but very sensible, and I think he could soon learn to gallop through the sky.'

'Right,' said Santa Claus, 'I'll give him a trial run with the others, a week before Christmas. Have my sleigh ready, and a sack of potatoes in it, instead of a sack of toys – just so that we have plenty of weight to pull.'

Well, on the Saturday before Christmas, the reindeer were harnessed to the sleigh. The new one, Quick-as-the-Wind, was very excited and proud. He kept tossing his head in delight, and his bells jingled loudly.

'Do keep still,' said the stable-man. 'And don't toss your head when you're in the sky – you might tear a cloud to pieces!'

'I hope there won't *be* any clouds in the sky,' said Santa Claus. 'If they're thick they may make me lose my way. Now then – are we ready? All you have to do, Quick-as-the-Wind, is to gallop in exact time with the others, and don't get out of step. Geeeeeee-UP!'

And away they went, galloping straight up in the sky, and then across it at top speed. It was a bright, starry night, but there was no moon. Quick-as-the-Wind was enjoying himself very much – how wonderful it was to gallop through the air! He threw up his head in delight, and all the bells on his antlers jingled loudly.

He tossed his head in joy again and again, and one of the bells became loose. At the next toss of his head the bell was jerked right off, and fell down, down, down through the air to the earth below. None of the reindeer knew it had gone, and Santa Claus didn't guess either.

Now, far down below, three children were looking out of their window before going to bed. Peter, who had ears as sharp as a dog, heard bells jingling quite clearly on the frosty air.

'Listen! Bells!' he said. 'It might be Christmas Eve, with Santa Claus galloping through the sky and reindeer bells jingling gaily.'

'Well, it *isn't* Christmas Eve!' said Dilys, looking up into the starry sky. Then she suddenly cried out in surprise and pointed upwards. 'Look – what's that passing across the sky – see, up there!'

The others looked intently, and sure enough they could *just* make out something passing swiftly across the stars! Was it an aeroplane? No, a plane would make a noise – and the only noise they could hear was the far-off sound of jingling!

'Strange!' said Thomas. 'Very strange. Whatever can it be?'

And then, just at that moment a little shining object fell into their garden. It didn't shine very brightly, but just caught the lamp-light from their window as it fell. The children heard a tiny thud, a little jingle, and then all was quiet.

'What was that?' said Peter, startled. 'Did you see something fall? I heard a little thud, too.'

'Yes. Let's go and see what it was,' said Dilys, suddenly excited. 'I say – could it have fallen from that thing we saw in the sky?'

'Well – I suppose it might have,' said Thomas,

scrambling down from the window-seat. 'Let's go and look for it!'

All three ran downstairs and into the garden. Peter took his torch with him and it wasn't long before they found the fallen reindeer bell. It was quite big, beautifully polished, and jingled loudly when Peter shook it.

'What a big bell!' he said. 'It's as big as our ping-pong ball. Wherever did it come from? No aeroplane would carry *bells*!'

'Let's go and show it to Mother,' said Dilys. So they went indoors and found their mother. 'Look,' said Dilys, 'this fell into our garden just now, Mother. A bell!'

'What a strange thing to happen!' said their mother, handling it. 'And see – it's got letters engraved on it!'

'Yes – two beautifully engraved letters,' said Peter. 'Look – that's an S. And this one's a C. Goodness – S.C.! I suppose they are the initials of the owner of the bell. It must be a very *important* bell.'

'S.C.,' said Thomas, slowly. 'My word – I wonder – no that's silly! It couldn't be!'

'*What* do you wonder?' asked Peter.

'Well – S.C. might stand for Santa Claus,' said Thomas. 'Mightn't it?'

The others stared at him, full of sudden excitement. 'That thing we saw jingling through the sky – it might have been a sleigh!' cried Dilys.

'But Santa Claus only rides out on Christmas Eve,' said Thomas.

'How do *you* know? He might take his reindeer for a run any time – he might want to make sure they knew their way for Christmas-time!' said Dilys. 'Oh, I'm absolutely *certain* it was Santa Claus and his reindeer! And one of the reindeer bells came loose and dropped off – into our garden!'

'Oh, darling – I don't really think such a thing could happen!' said her mother, laughing. 'Though it certainly is strange that the bell has those initials on it.'

'Mother – it must be a very *lucky* bell if it belongs to Santa Claus,' said Peter. 'Perhaps it will bring us good luck. Oh, I wish Daddy was here, too, to hear about this. He won't be home for Christmas, will he?'

'I'm afraid not,' said his mother. 'He's a thousand miles away! We'll have to manage without him this Christmas.'

Dilys took the bell into her hand and warmed it. 'Bell – you must be very, very lucky,' she said. 'Bring us luck this week, please. Let's have lots of lovely presents for Christmas! Do try and be lucky, bell!'

'What are we going to do with it?' asked Peter. 'We ought to try to find the owner, if it isn't Santa Claus.'

'It's his bell, I'm sure it is!' said Dilys. 'It *must* have fallen off one of his galloping reindeer!'

'Well – we could always put it up on the roof, lighted by a little lamp!' said Thomas, with a laugh. 'Then if he comes to *our* house on Christmas Eve, he'll be sure to see it, and take it away!'

'Oh, yes – let's do that when Christmas comes!'

said Dilys. 'We'll know Santa Claus has been, if the bell is gone!'

The children put the bell in the middle of the sitting-room mantelpiece, and looked at it a dozen times a day. Dilys kept rubbing it and wishing with it. She said that she was so sure it was a lucky bell that she wanted to make the most of it every minute she could!

But somehow that bell *didn't* bring them luck! In fact, a lot of horrid things happened that week. First of all the presents sent to them for Christmas by their father didn't arrive. 'They must have been lost on the way,' said Mother. 'They should have been here by now.'

And then Mother had a *big* piece of bad luck! She lost her purse! She took it out shopping with her to buy a big chicken for Christmas Day, a Christmas tree, lots of presents, and other things. She had pushed her bag into her shopping-basket – and then when she put down her hand for it – it was gone!

'Somebody must have taken it!' said Mother, in a panic. 'Oh, and I had such a lot of money in it! Peter, Dilys, Thomas – it was our Christmas money. Now we shan't be able to have half the things I wanted you to have!'

'Poor Mother!' said Thomas. 'I'll go to the police-station and report it. Perhaps it dropped out of your basket. If so, someone may bring it back.'

But nobody did. It had been stolen. What bad luck, just in Christmas week! The children were very sad because they had so much looked forward to a good time at Christmas – but they were so sorry for their mother that they didn't make any fuss at all!

Then Dilys caught a dreadful cold and had to go to bed. She scowled at the bell as she went upstairs. 'Horrid bell! Unlucky bell! Nothing has gone right since we found it. For goodness' sake let's get rid of it, Thomas. Be sure to put it up on the roof so that Santa Claus can take the horrid thing away!'

Well, on Christmas Eve when Santa Claus went

out in his sleigh, he was indeed astonished to see his lost reindeer bell gleaming in the light of a little lamp, up on the roof of the children's house! Thomas had gone up to the loft, opened the skylight there, and put out the bell and the lamp. There they were, waiting for Santa Claus, at about half-past eleven on Christmas Eve!

'Well! If that isn't the bell Quick-as-the-Wind lost last week!' said Santa Claus. 'Now who found it – and how kind to put it up here for me to take! I've a good mind to knock at the front door and find out if the children's parents are still up. I see there is a light downstairs.'

The children's mother was most astonished to hear someone knocking at the front door. A voice said, 'Don't be alarmed. It's only Santa Claus. I've just found my reindeer bell on the roof.'

'Oh! Do come in!' called the mother, and opened the door to Santa Claus. 'I'm still busy trying to finish some little presents for the children,' she said. 'We had some bad luck this week. The children hoped that your reindeer bell might be a lucky one – but it wasn't!'

'Hmm!' said Santa Claus. 'I'm sorry about that. Our bells are neither lucky *nor* unlucky – just bells. But maybe *I'm* a bit lucky! What were you going to buy with the money you lost?'

'Oh – the usual things,' said the mother. 'A good plump chicken, a Christmas cake, decorations, and chocolates and sweets and fruit – and presents, of course!'

'You leave all that to me, and get to bed,' said Santa Claus, kindly. 'You look tired out. Where's your husband? Can't he help?'

'He's a thousand miles away!' said the mother, with a sigh. 'Oh dear – you *are* kind – and I haven't even offered you anything to eat or drink. Are you cold – would you like some cocoa or hot milk?'

'No thank you,' said Santa Claus. 'I would *like* to say yes – but this is my busy night, you know. Now – will you please leave all this work you're doing, and go to bed? I've something to do here that I don't want you to see. Goodnight – and a very happy Christmas!'

The mother went upstairs in a daze. Could it *really* be true that Santa Claus himself had come knocking at the door so late at night? And he had actually found that bell up on the roof! How wonderful!

Santa Claus became very busy when the mother had gone. Strange noises came from the sitting-room and the kitchen. One of the noises was made by Santa Claus – he hummed quietly to himself because he was feeling very pleased. How pleasant to bring a little good luck to such a nice family!

The reindeer waiting outside couldn't *imagine* why he was so long. They stamped their hooves, and jingled their bells impatiently. It was a wonder that the sleeping children didn't hear them!

Santa Claus came out at last, very hot, very happy and in a great hurry. He clambered into his sleigh and shook the reins. 'Make haste now!' he said.

'We've lost a lot of time – you must gallop twice as fast as usual!' And away they went, jingling through the sky!

The children awoke about seven o'clock next morning. It was Peter who saw the wonderful sight first. He gave a loud shout. 'Dilys! Thomas! Look at all this!'

What a marvellous sight they saw! Toys of all kinds were piled here and there – their stockings were full to the top – and in a separate corner, on an armchair, was a pile of things marked '*For your mother.*'

'A woolly coat, stockings, a new electric kettle, a box of chocolates – I say, look at all these lovely things for Mother. Whatever does it all mean?' cried Dilys. 'Mother, Mother, come here!'

'Oh!' said Mother, coming quickly into the bedroom.

'*Oh!* Good gracious! So this is what Santa Claus was busy about after I went to bed!'

'Santa Claus! What do you mean, Mother? Did he

come? Did he find the bell? Mother, what's it all about?' cried Peter.

'I'll just go and light the fire downstairs, then I'll tell you all about it!' said Mother – but no sooner was she downstairs than she called back in excitement. 'Come down here – just come down here!'

Down rushed the three children – and stared in amazement at the sitting-room. It was beautifully decorated – and in the corner was a lovely Christmas tree, hung with ornaments and parcels. Tins of biscuits and boxes of chocolates, and all kinds of fruit were on the sideboard – and in the larder was a fine turkey, ready to roast, and all kinds of goodies.

'Did – did Santa Claus do all this?' asked Peter, in wonder. 'Why? I don't understand it. How did he know we hadn't much for Christmas?'

'I'll tell you,' said his mother, and soon they had all heard how Santa Claus had come knocking at the door the night before, after he had found his reindeer bell on the roof.

'I *wish* I'd seen him, Mother!' said Dilys, longingly. '*Why* didn't you wake us? If only I'd heard him knock-knock-knocking...'

Knock, knock, knock! Was that Santa Claus at the door again? Someone was there, knocking loudly. It must be old Santa Claus! Now they could thank him!

But it wasn't Santa Claus – it was their father! There he was, beaming at them. 'I got sudden leave and flew home!' he said. 'And a funny journey it was, too – I thought I heard jingling bells all the way!'

Jingling bells! Now what was the meaning of *that*? But there was no time to explain anything, everyone wanted to hug and be hugged. And who minded if Daddy hadn't had time to bring them any special presents?

'*You're* our best Christmas present!' cried Dilys. 'Oh, why did we say that bell was unlucky? It was the luckiest find we *ever, ever* had!'

Christmas Carols

A Family Christmas
Part Eight:

Christmas Carols

'WE OUGHT really to dance while we sing the Christmas carols,' said Daddy, 'because the word "carol" means a ring-dance, a dance in a circle.'

'Did people dance in the churches in olden days then!' said Susan, astonished. 'Did they sing and dance at the same time?'

'Oh yes,' said Daddy. 'That was an old, old religious custom, which began long before Christ was born. Then, when the early Christians took over some of the old customs, and made them into Christian rites, singing and dancing was allowed in their churches too.'

'But we don't dance in church now,' said Benny.

'No, because it was forbidden years and years ago,' said his father. 'The word "carol" soon came to mean a merry song suggestive of dancing, a happy song, bringing in such things as the Nativity, or the shepherds or angels. We like to sing them at Christmas time because it is a happy time, and we want merry, dancing tunes then.'

'I suppose our carols are very old,' said Susan.

'A good many of them are,' said Daddy. 'The man who really began the true carol was St Francis of Assisi, who was born in the twelfth century.'

'I know about St Francis,' said Ann. 'I've got a picture of him in my bedroom. He called Jesus our "Little Brother". Did St Francis make up some of our carols?'

'We don't know for certain,' said her father, 'but probably some of his companions did. Then, from Italy, where St Francis lived, the carol spread abroad, keeping its simplicity, religious feeling and merry spirit. There is another kind of carol we know too – the ones we call the "Nowells".'

'Oh yes – there's "The First Noël", said Ann. 'We'll sing it tonight – won't we, Mummy?'

'We know a very popular carol that came from Bohemia,' said Daddy, 'all about a good king of Bohemia. Who knows the carol I mean?'

'Good King Wenceslas,' said all the children at once.

'Right,' said their father. 'He was a real king, and his feast is held on St Stephen's Day, which is Boxing Day.'

'Boxing Day!' said Benny. 'Now what does *that* mean, Daddy? It has always seemed to be such a funny name for the day after Christmas. Do people go and watch boxing matches somewhere?'

They all laughed. 'Of course not, silly,' said Susan. 'It's because the postman and the dustman used to come round for their Christmas boxes, isn't it, Daddy?'

'Yes, it is,' said Daddy.

'But we don't give them boxes, we give them money,' said Anne, puzzled. 'Did they used to get boxes instead?'

'No,' said Daddy. 'What happened was this – boxes were put into the churches for people to put money into to give to the poor. These boxes were opened on Christmas Day, and the next day the money was given to anyone in need.'

'Oh – so the day after Christmas was Box Money Day,' said Benny.

'Yes,' said Daddy, 'and in later years young apprentices took boxes round to their masters' customers, begging for money gifts, however small. The customers put money into these boxes – which, in those days were made of earthenware or porcelain, and could only be opened by being broken – and then the youngsters divided the money among themselves.'

'Well, it's easy to see how Boxing Day came to have its name then,' said Benny, 'with boxes for the poor in the churches, and boxes being taken round by apprentices. Our postman doesn't bring a box, though. And he doesn't come on Boxing Day.'

'Yes – and even when the whole custom has completely died out, we shall still call the day after Christmas "Boxing Day",' said Mummy. 'Always there are fingers of the past reaching out to us who live in the present.'

There came the sound of footsteps outside, and voices talking low. Then suddenly a carol was begun, and the family heard the sound of "Good King Wenceslas" being vigorously sung. The carol-singers had arrived.

Good King Wenceslas last look'd out
On the feast of Stephen;
When the snow lay round about,
Deep and crisp, and even . . .

The children joined in too, and then waited for the next carol. What was it to be?

'The first Nowell the angels did say,' began the

clear young voices. Ann smiled. 'They've chosen a Nowell,' she whispered. 'Let's sing it too.'

So they did. After that there came a knock at the door. Mother opened it. 'We're collecting for Age Concern,' said a voice. 'Please can you spare something?'

Mother gave them some money. The carol singers were pleased. They thanked her and went off to the next house.

'That is another very, very old custom,' said Daddy, 'singing carols for charity. Even as far back as Norman times carol singers went out at Christmas-time, and asked for money.'

'Well, now let *us* sing some, sitting round the blazing Yule log,' said Susan, her face glowing in the heat. 'I think this is nice, this custom of ours – sitting round a blazing log fire on Christmas Eve, all of us together, singing carols, and then listening to the old, old story.'

'We'll each choose a carol, as we always do,' said Mother. 'I'll choose "Hark, the Herald Angels Sing".

I hope you all know the words.'

Then ringing through the house went the six voices, Ann's a little out of tune, but just as loud as anyone else's.

Hark! the Herald Angels sing,
Glory to the New-born King;

'That was lovely,' said Susan, when the carol was finished. 'I do like carols. They are so merry and the tune makes you want to dance. Now what shall we have?'

'Let's have "I Saw Three Ships Come Sailing in,"' said Ann. So they sang it heartily.

Then Peter had his turn, and he chose 'The First Nowell the Angel did say'.

One by one they each chose a carol, and struck up the tunes. All the children knew the words well – even Ann – for they had sung them at school, and had learnt them properly. It was a very Christmassy evening.

When everyone had chosen his or her carol there was a silence. Mummy looked at the clock.

'It's getting a bit late,' she said.

'Well, we're not going to bed without our Christmas story,' said Peter, at once. Mum, you wouldn't break *our* old custom, would you? You've told us the Christmas story now every Christmas Eve without a stop. I don't remember a Christmas Eve when we haven't all been sitting cosily round the fire like this, listening to you.'

'Well, you shall once again,' said his mother, smiling round at the family, whose faces were all glowing in the light of the burning Yule log. 'It's a story you all know well, and have heard many many times, but everyone should hear it or read it again at Christmas-time, because it is such a beautiful tale.'

'We're ready,' said Peter, slipping down on to the hearth-rug. 'Begin, Mum.'

So Mother began the old story, about the birth of Jesus, in her low, clear voice, and all the family listened.

There was a silence after Mother had finished telling the story. Nobody spoke for quite a minute. The Yule log sent up a shower of sparks, and the children watched them. Then Ann gave a deep sigh.

'Thank you, Mummy. You do tell the Christmas story well – you make it so real. You make me feel as if I want to be one of the shepherds peeping into the stable – or even one of the wise men's servants peering over his master's shoulder just to get a glimpse of the little Jesus.'

'It is a wonderful old story,' said Benny, his eyes shining. 'I don't mind how many times I hear it, when it is told like you tell it, Mum. I wish I had been on the hillside with the shepherds.'

'It will soon be Jesus's birthday,' said Susan. 'It's nice to think that although we can't give *Him* presents, we can give other people gifts instead. We keep His birthday that way.'

The clock struck, and Ann and Peter frowned at it. It always struck just at the wrong time and reminded Mummy that it was getting late.

It reminded her now. 'Time for your supper,' she said. 'Then you must hang up your stockings and go to bed. Otherwise you will certainly not be asleep when Santa Claus comes.'

'Oh, Mummy – would you tell us the story of Santa Claus himself, before we go?' begged Peter.

'Certainly not,' said Mother. 'To begin with there's no time left, and to end with, I don't know anything about him, I'm afraid.'

'Do you, Daddy?' asked Susan. Her father shook his head.

'Well no, I don't,' he said. 'I don't even know how he got his name, or why he comes, or anything. Anyway, I really think you know enough about Christmas-time now. Come and have your suppers.'

They all sat down at the table. They were hungry. Ann and Peter were very sleepy, for it was long past their usual bedtime.

'Now, upstairs all of you,' said Mummy. 'And I'm sure I need hardly remind you to – hang your stockings up!'

The Very
Full Stocking

The Very
Full Stocking

ONCE UPON a time there was a fat kitten called Fluffy. He lived in a little house with his mother and father, and had a lovely time. They spoilt him dreadfully, because he was their only kitten, so he had all the cream that was on the top of the milk, plenty of sardines, and half of his mother's kipper at supper-time.

Now one Christmas night he was very excited. His mother had promised that he should hang up his stocking and that in the morning he would find it filled with all kinds of good things.

'But you must go to sleep quickly, or you will find

your stocking empty in the morning,' said his mother.

He went to sleep quickly. He didn't hear the tiny mouse that lived in the hole of the wall come creeping out. He didn't hear the mouse sniffing to see if there were any crumbs on the floor.

The tiny mouse was hungry. The cats didn't leave very much for him to nibble, and he was always terribly afraid of being caught. He came out each night, and sometimes he was lucky enough to find a crumb or two, and sometimes he wasn't.

Tonight he smelt a most delicious smell. It was the smell of cheese, sardines, kipper, and lots of other things. Wherever could they be?

The little mouse ran to the end of Fluffy's cot. Good gracious! The smell came from there! The mouse stood up on his back legs and sniffed harder.

'What a strange thing!' thought the mouse. 'Fluffy's stocking is crammed full of delicious things tonight! Never before has there been anything in his stockings – but tonight one of them is quite full. If only I could creep up and have a nibble!'

Well, it didn't take him long to clamber up the bed-clothes on to the cot. He ran to where the stocking was hanging on the foot of the cot, and stood up to sniff.

But alas for the poor little mouse! He stood on one of Fluffy's paws! And, of course, that woke up Fluffy at once. Fluffy sat up, wondering who was treading on him – and in a trice he flicked out his paw and caught the trembling mouse!

'Let me go, let me go!' squeaked the mouse in fright.

'What were you doing on my bed?' asked the kitten.

'Only smelling at all the good things in your stocking,' said the mouse. 'That's all. It's a wonderful stocking you have tonight.'

'Is it?' cried Fluffy in surprise, and he too began to sniff. 'Dear me, yes – my stocking is full of the most delicious things to eat. How *dare* you come and sniff at my Christmas stocking, Mouse?'

'I'm very sorry,' said the mouse. 'But it's such a

marvellous stocking I couldn't help it. Please do let me go.'

'I'll let you go if you can do something impossible,' said Fluffy with a chuckle, for, like all cats, he loved to tease mice.

'What's that?' asked the mouse in fear.

'Well, you see my stocking, don't you?' said the kitten. 'Now, it's quite crammed full – there's not a corner to push in anything else. If you can put something else in my stocking, you may go free! If you can't, I'll eat you for breakfast.'

The little mouse thought hard, his heart beating fast. Then a fine idea came into his tiny head.

'I *can* put in something else,' he said.

'You can't,' said the kitten scornfully. 'Why, not even I could – so I'm sure *you* couldn't.'

'I can,' said the mouse.

'All right. Go on – try,' said the kitten, and he took his paw off the little mouse. The mouse ran to the stocking. He stood up on his hind legs and nibbled away at the bottom of the stocking, at the toe. He nibbled and he nibbled.

'What are you doing?' said the kitten angrily. 'That's not putting anything else in my stocking.'

'Wait,' said the mouse. 'Wait.' And he nibbled again at the toe.

'Mouse, stop nibbling,' cried the kitten. 'You are spoiling my stocking. Unless you tell me at once what you are going to put into it, I'll catch you again!'

'Kitten, use your brains,' said the mouse cheekily. 'I have put something into your stocking that wasn't there before – I have put a hole there! There's always room for a hole, no matter how full a stocking is!'

And without waiting to see what Fluffy would say, the mouse leaped off the cot, ran to his hole and disappeared. Fluffy was angry.

'Putting a hole into my stocking!' he said. 'What next! Bad little mouse! I'll eat him next time I see him!'

But he didn't get the chance, for as soon as Fluffy was fast asleep once more, the mouse came creeping from his hole with two big bags. He went to the end of the cot and, standing on the floor, he waited for the things in the stocking to fall through the hole he had made at the end.

A bit of kipper fell through. That went into the mouse's bag. A whole sardine fell out, and then a piece of cream cheese. Those went into the bags too, and soon they were quite full.

The mouse gave a squeak of delight and ran back to his hole. He put on his new hat, tied a scarf round his neck, for it was a frosty night, and set out to find a new and safer hole, carrying with him enough food to stock a nice big mouse-larder for a week!

I don't know where he went to – but I can't help hoping that such a clever little creature found a good home, and lived happily ever after!

In Santa Claus's Castle

In Santa Claus's Castle

In this adventure from The Enchanted wood, *Joe, Beth and Frannie are stuck in the Land of Toys with Moon-Face, Saucepan and Silky the Fairy. They have been turned into toys themselves, and Silky is nearly captured by Mr Oom-Boom-Boom, a spell-maker they go to for help. Joe has tied the man to a table with his own beard, and the six of them are making their escape ...*

JOE GOT to the car first. 'Quick!' he cried. 'I can hear Oom-Boom-Boom coming! He must have got free.'

So he had! He appeared at the door of his peculiar house, and they saw that he had freed himself by cutting his beard short. He did look strange.

The toy rabbit revved up his car and it shot off, almost before Saucepan was safely in. A kettle flew, clanging, down the road, and Saucepan groaned.

'Well, thank goodness that kettle's gone,' said Joe. 'It can't stick into me again. Oh, dear – I feel I want to turn head-over-heels.'

'Well, you can't,' said Moon-Face firmly. 'Unless you want to be caught by the Oom-Boom-Boom fellow. Here, Saucepan, hang on to Joe, and stop him turning head-over-heels in the car!'

It was difficult to stop him, but they managed it. After they had gone a good way the rabbit stopped the car for a talk, and Joe took the chance of turning about a dozen somersaults.

'You know, I think you should go to the Land of Santa Claus,' said the rabbit. 'I do really. Not to give him Silky, of course, that would never do – but to tell him you aren't toys and to ask him if he can stop you being what you're not.'

'That's a bit muddling,' said Moon-Face, trying to work it out. 'Yes – it seems a good idea. After all, he deals in toys, doesn't he? He must know them very well. He'll be able to tell we're not real toys, and *might* help us.'

'We know he's kind,' said Silky. 'He's so fond of children. Let's go to him. How can we get there, though? This land may stay at the top of the Faraway Tree for some time – and the Land of Santa Claus may not be the next one to arrive.'

'That's true enough,' said the rabbit. 'Actually the next land on the timetable is the Land of Squalls, which doesn't sound too good. But I'll tell you what I can do for you!'

'What?' asked Joe.

'I can drive you to the next station and put you on a train for the Land of Santa Claus,' said the toy rabbit. 'I happened to notice that some trains there do go to his land. What about it, friends?'

'A very good idea,' said everyone, and off they

went. They came to a funny little station after a while, and they all got out.

'I wish you could stay in my land for ever, Silky doll,' said the rabbit to Silky. 'You really are the prettiest thing I ever saw. But there – you'd be unhappy and I couldn't bear that.'

'I'll write to you,' said Silky.

'Will you really?' said the rabbit. 'Do you know, I've never had a letter in my life! It *would* make me feel important! Look, there's a train in!'

'Wow! This train's going to the Land of Santa Claus! What a bit of luck!' cried Moon-Face. 'Goodbye, rabbit. You really have been a good friend. I'll write to you.'

'My goodness – fancy me getting two letters!' said the delighted rabbit.

'We'll *all* write,' said Joe, shaking his furry hand warmly. 'Goodbye. It's been lovely meeting you.'

Silky gave him a kiss and he nearly cried for joy. 'I've never been kissed before,' he said. 'Never. A kiss

– and letters – my goodness, I am a lucky rabbit!'

They all climbed into the train and waved goodbye.

'Nice fellow, that rabbit,' said Joe. 'Well, we're off again. I wonder how far it is.'

It was quite a long way, and they all fell asleep. A porter woke them up at last. 'Hey, you! Don't you want to get out here?' he said. 'This is where toys usually get out.'

They scrambled out because the station board said, 'Get out here for the Castle of Santa Claus!'

'Just in time,' said Joe, yawning. 'Oh – here I go, turning head-over-heels again!'

'There's the castle – look!' said Beth, pointing to a magnificent castle with many towers, rising high on a hill nearby. 'And, goodness – look at the snow! Anyone would think it was winter here.'

'Oh, it always is,' said the porter. 'It wouldn't be much good for sleighs, would it, if there wasn't snow? Is Santa Claus expecting you? His sleigh usually meets the train in case there are any visitors for him.'

'Is that it down there?' asked Moon-Face, pointing down into the snowy station yard. A sleigh was there, with four lovely reindeer, whose bells jingled as they moved restlessly. A small red pixie held the reins.

'Yes, that's the sleigh. Better go and get in,' said the porter. He stared hard at Silky. 'Goodness, isn't that a pretty doll? I bet Santa Claus will want her for his own Christmas tree.'

They went to the sleigh and got into it. 'To Santa Claus, please,' said Joe, and off they went, gliding smoothly over the snow, drawn by the four eager reindeer.

They arrived at the castle. They felt rather nervous when they saw how big and grand it was. They stood at an enormous door, carved with all kinds of toys, and rang a great bell.

The door swung open. 'Please come in,' said a teddy bear, dressed like a footman. 'Santa Claus will see you in a few minutes.'

They went into a big hall and then into a great

room, where many little pixies and goblins were at work. 'You might like to look round while you're waiting,' said the bear footman. 'You'll see the pixies painting the dolls' houses, and the goblins putting growls into us bears, and you'll see how the somersaults are put into the clockwork clowns.'

'I don't want to see that,' said Joe, feeling at once that he wanted to go head-over-heels. He turned a few and then stood up again. 'What are those pixies doing over there?' he said.

'Putting the hum into tops,' said the footman. 'But don't go too near. One of the hums might get into you by mistake, and that's *such* a nuisance, you know!'

They stood at a safe distance, watching. It was very interesting indeed. So many things were going on; there was so much to see and hear, that they almost forgot they were toys themselves.

'How's your growl, bear?' said a little pixie, running up to Moon-Face. He pressed him in the middle and

Moon-Face growled deeply. 'Grrrrr! Leave me alone! I don't like people doing that. Grrrrr!'

'Look – oh, look – isn't that Santa Claus himself?' cried Beth, suddenly, as a big man came into the room dressed in bright red. He wore a hood trimmed with white, and his jolly face had eyes that twinkled brightly.

'Yes. It's Santa Claus!' cried Joe. Santa Claus heard him and came over at once. He looked in surprise at Silky.

'Why!' he said, 'where did you come from? *You* weren't made in my castle, by pixies and goblins. You are the loveliest doll I've ever seen. I've a good mind to keep you for myself and put you at the very top of my own big Christmas tree.'

'No, no, please not!' said Silky. Santa Claus looked down at the others. He seemed puzzled.

'Where do you all come from?' he said. 'I am quite sure I have never had any toys made like you. The rabbit, dressed up in kettles and saucepans, for instance – and this funny little bear. He doesn't seem like a proper teddy.'

'We're *not* proper toys!' said Beth. 'Santa Claus, we got turned into toys in the fort of the toy soldiers. I'm a little girl really.'

'And I'm Moon-Face, who lives at the top of the Faraway Tree,' said Moon-Face.

'What! The famous Moon-Face, who has a slippery-slip in his room, going down the tree from the top to the bottom!' cried Santa Claus. 'My goodness – I've often wanted to see that! Do you think I'm too fat to go down it?'

'No – no, I don't think so,' said Moon-Face, looking at him. 'I could give you *two* cushions to sit on instead of one. If you'd like to come now, you can go up and down the Faraway Tree as often as you like – we'll haul you up in the washing basket every time you arrive at the bottom, and you can slide down again from the top!'

'Let's go now,' said Santa Claus in delight. 'Well,

well – to think I'm meeting the famous Moon-Face at last! And I suppose this lovely doll is Silky the fairy. And, of course – this is the Old Saucepan Man!'

'But – how do you know us?' asked Moon-Face, astonished.

'Oh, I've heard about you from the children,' said Santa Claus. 'They keep asking me for books about you, to go into their Christmas stockings and they looked so exciting that I read them all. I *did* want to meet you!'

Well, wasn't that a bit of luck? Santa Claus called his sleigh and they all got in. 'To the top of the Faraway Tree,' commanded Santa Claus, and away they went. It didn't take very long. In quite a little while the sleigh landed on a broad bough near the top of the tree, and they all got out.

'My room is just a bit higher up,' said Moon-Face, and led the way. They were soon in his little round room. He pointed to the curious hole in the middle of the floor.

'There you are,' he said. 'That's the slippery-slip – it goes round and round from top to bottom of the tree – and you fly out of the trapdoor at the bottom, and land on a soft cushion of moss.'

'Splendid!' said Santa Claus. 'Will somebody else go first, please? Goodness, it's exactly the same as I read about in the books!'

'Er – do you think you could just change us back to our ordinary selves?' asked Joe, afraid that in his excitement Santa Claus might forget to do what they so badly wanted. 'I feel as if I'm going to somersault again, and I don't want to turn head-over-heels all the way down the slippery-slip.'

'Change you back? Yes, of course; it's easy!' said Santa Claus. 'The slippery-slip is just the right place for a spell. Shut your eyes, please.'

They all shut their eyes. Santa Claus touched each one gently, chanting a curious little song:

'Go in as you are,

Come out as you were,

Go in as you are,
Come out as you were!'

They opened their eyes. Moon-Face got a cushion and pulled Beth on to it. He gave her a tremendous push and she shot down the slippery-slip at top speed – round and round – and then out she flew through the trapdoor at the bottom, and landed on a tuft of moss.

'Oh,' she said, breathless. 'Oh! I'm myself again. I'm not a stiff-jointed doll any longer – and I can shut and open my eyes properly!'

She got up – and out of the trapdoor flew Joe. 'Joe! You're all right again! You're you!' cried Beth in delight. 'And here comes Silky – she's not a doll any more – and here's Frannie – she's all right, too. Look out – here's the Old Saucepan Man – yippee, he's back to normal!'

'And he's lost his floppy ears,' said Silky. 'I'm rather sorry. I liked him with those long ears. Good old Saucepan.'

And then, WhoooooOOOOOOSH! The trapdoor

shot open with a bang and out sailed Santa Claus, his hood on the back of his head! Bump! He went on to the cushion of moss, and sat there, panting and full of delight.

'What a thrill! WHAT a thrill! Better than anything I've got in my castle.'

'Look out! Here comes Moon-Face!' cried Joe, and out came Moon-Face, no longer a fat teddy bear, but his own beaming self once more.

'I'd like to do that again,' said Santa Claus, standing up. 'How did you say we got back to the top of the tree? In a basket?'

'Yes,' said Joe, 'but if you don't mind, we won't come with the others. You see, our mother will be wondering about us. So we'd better say goodbye and thank you very much.'

'Goodbye. See you next Christmas,' said Santa Claus. 'I'll bring you something extra nice. Ah – here comes the basket, let down on a rope. Do we get in?'

The last thing that Joe, Beth and Frannie saw was

Santa Claus in the big basket, being pulled slowly up by all the squirrels at the top of the tree. Moon-Face and Silky and Saucepan were with him, leaning over the edge of the basket, waving to them.

'Well – I suppose dear old Santa Claus will be going down that slippery-slip till it's dark,' said Joe. 'Oh dear – surely I'm not going to turn head-over-heels again! I feel just like it!'

'Oh, you'll soon get out of the habit,' said Beth. 'I still feel as if I want to walk stiffly like a doll. Goodness, wasn't that an adventure!'

'We'll never have a better one,' said Frannie.

Oh yes, you will, Frannie, Beth and Joe. You just wait and see!

A Visitor in
the Night

A Visitor in the Night

'I'M GOING to hang up my longest stocking,' said Susan, and she took out a very long one indeed, with no holes in it.

'I've borrowed one of Daddy's,' said Ann. 'My socks are too small.'

Peter and Benny hung up football socks. 'Quite a collection of stockings for Santa Claus to fill,' said Benny.

'I know you don't believe in Santa Claus, but I do,' said Ann, getting into bed, and calling through the door to Benny. 'I'm going to wait up and ask him about himself. I want to know *his* story too. He must have got one!'

'You'll never keep awake!' said Susan, jumping into her bed.

'Here's Mummy to say goodnight,' said Ann. 'Mummy, who first thought of hanging up Christmas stockings? It's such a good idea!'

'I don't know,' said Mummy. 'I only know that French and Dutch children used to put out their wooden shoes – their sabots – on Christmas Eve for presents to be put into them. So I suppose hanging up stockings came from much the same idea. Now – no more Christmas questions, Ann. Go to sleep, and wake up in the morning to find your stocking full from top to toe. But no getting out of bed until seven o'clock!'

Mummy said goodnight to everyone, and turned out the lights. Benny and Peter fell asleep at once. Susan gave the little twitches she always did when she was almost asleep. She didn't answer when Ann spoke to her.

'Susan. Are you asleep?'

A VISITOR IN THE NIGHT

Ann lay quietly in her bed. It was quite dark. She didn't feel at all sleepy. She lay and wondered about Santa Claus. Who was he really? Why did he come secretly at Christmas time? Why didn't he like people to see him?

'I wish I *could* stay awake and see Santa Claus,' she thought. 'I don't feel a bit sleepy. But I suppose I ought to go to sleep. I'll try.'

She tried very hard. She screwed up her eyes, but they soon opened again, and looked into the darkness. She could hear Susan's steady breathing in the bed nearby.

'I'll make up a story in my mind,' thought Ann. 'That's a good way to make myself go to sleep.'

But she seemed wider awake than ever. Then she heard Daddy winding up the clock downstairs. That meant that he and Mummy were coming up to bed too. Goodness, it must be terribly late!

The clock in the hall struck loudly – just once. 'It's half-past something,' said Ann. 'Half-past ten or maybe half-past eleven. I don't know which. Oh – here come Daddy and Mummy.'

She sat up as her mother came softly into the room. She saw Ann looking at her and she was not very pleased.

'Ann! Not asleep yet? It's terribly late. Lie down at once.'

Ann lay down with a sigh. Her mother and father went into their own room and Ann heard them talking in low voices. Then there was the creak of the bed. Daddy and Mother would soon be asleep. Ann would be the only one awake.

The grandfather clock downstairs ticked on through the night very loudly. Ann listened to him. He struck again – twelve times. So it was twelve o'clock. Midnight!

Ann turned over and shut her eyes again. Then she heard a noise in the distance that made her open her eyes with a jerk.

She heard bells. What a funny thing to hear in the middle of the night. They were not church bells – they were jingly bells.

Jingle-jingle-jingle, went the bells, coming nearer and nearer. Then there came a soft scraping noise up on the roof, and a low voice spoke. Ann couldn't hear what was said. The bells jingled once or twice more and then stopped.

Ann's heart beat very fast. She felt quite certain that Santa Claus had arrived. Those bells were the bells of his reindeer – that scraping noise was the sleigh landing on the roof. That low voice was the voice of Santa Claus himself.

The little girl slipped out of bed and went to the window to look out. She could only see the whiteness of the thick snow. As she looked out she heard a curious sound overhead.

'Exactly like a reindeer stamping a hoof on thick snow up on the roof,' thought Ann, her heart beating faster. 'Oh, I *know* it's Santa Claus. He's come. I wonder which chimney he'll come down.'

She thought for a moment. 'I think it will be the very big chimney we have in the lounge – the one we have been burning the Yule-log in tonight. I'll go down and hide myself and watch.'

The little girl put on her dressing-gown and slippers, for the night was very cold. She opened her bedroom door quietly and crept out into the passage. Down the stairs she went, as quietly as she could, and came at last to the half-open door of the lounge. The Yule log was still alight, so there was a glow from the fireplace.

No one was there – but what was that noise in the chimney? Ann's knees began to shake a little. It was all very well to keep awake like this and hope to see Santa Claus – but what would he say if he saw her? He might be very cross.

She hid behind the sofa and waited. The noise in the chimney went on – and then, to Ann's great excitement, a big pair of legs appeared down the great chimney-place of the hearth. They wore large-sized black boots. A grunting noise came down the chimney at the same time as the boots. Then, neatly avoiding the still-burning log, a stout red-clad body came down the chimney and landed on the hearth among the fire-irons. They made a little clatter.

Ann peeped above the sofa. Yes, it really and truly was Santa Claus. There was no mistake about it at all. He was dressed in red, and had a red hood over his head, edged with white fur. On his hands were enormous fur gloves. His face was red and plump and jolly, and his beard was as white as the snow outside.

Ann didn't feel a bit afraid of him when she saw his cheerful, jolly face. Santa Claus looked round the room, brushed his tunic with his hand, and sat down with a sigh on a chair by the fire.

'I'm getting too fat for chimneys,' Ann heard him say. Then he looked at the fire and gave the log a little kick with his boot, that made it flare up at once. The fire-light flickered all over the room.

A jingling noise sounded, and Santa Claus got up at once and called up the chimney.

'Now then, Swift-One, stand still. You'll set

the others fidgeting if you start!'

The jingling stopped. Santa Claus sat down again. Smoke blew out of the fire-place and he coughed. He looked round and gave an exclamation of annoyance.

'Left my sack in the chimney again. Now the fire will begin to smoke!'

He knelt down by the burning log, and thrust his great arm up the warm chimney. He pulled down a sack quite full of something.

'Toys,' thought Ann, her eyes shining. 'His sack of toys. What a nice, kind, generous old man he is. Oh, how I wish I could give *him* a present!'

Ann suddenly thought of a bottle of sweets she had. She had bought it with her own money, meaning to give it to her aunt, but then she had seen a handkerchief with her aunt's name in the corner – Mary – and she had bought that instead. So she had the bottle of sweets and no one to give it to – but she could give it to Santa Claus!

The sweets were in a nearby cupboard. Ann crawled

to it and opened the door. She took out the sweets. Then trembling, stood up and spoke.

'Good evening, Santa Claus!'

Santa Claus gave an enormous jump and looked round, startled. He saw Ann, in her blue dressing-gown, standing near to him, looking rather scared.

'Bless us all!' he said, in a deep voice, 'what a fright you gave me.'

'Santa Claus, you're always giving other people presents, and now I've got one for *you*,' said Ann, and she held out the bottle of boiled sweets. Santa Claus took it and smiled.

'My favourite sweets – and plenty of red ones too – how lovely. Thank you, little girl – no one has ever given *me* a present before. Did you hear me come down the chimney?'

'Yes – and I heard the jingling of your reindeers' harness and bells,' said Ann. 'Oh Santa Claus, it's simply marvellous to see you. Are you real? I'm not dreaming, am I?'

'How am I to know if you're dreaming or not?' said Santa Claus.

'Well – my sister and brothers would know if I am dreaming,' said Ann, an idea coming into her head. 'Could I go and get them and let them see you? If they can see you, I shall know I'm not dreaming.'

'Fetch them, then,' said Santa Claus. 'Is that lemonade I see on the side-board there? Could I have some, do you think? I feel very thirsty.'

'Oh Santa Claus – would you like some sandwiches, or biscuits – and some hot cocoa?' said Ann. 'Susan – that's my sister – can make lovely cocoa. We could all have some together, and talk to you. We'd like to ask you lots of questions.'

Santa Claus pulled out an enormous gold watch. 'Well,' he said, 'I've got a little time to spare – and hot cocoa and biscuits and a talk do sound rather nice. Go and fetch your sister and brothers, find out whether you are dreaming or not, and then let's have a cosy time together.'

Ann was so happy. She sped upstairs and into her own bedroom. She went to Susan and pulled her arm.

'Susan! Wake up. Quick, wake up. There's a visitor downstairs.'

Susan woke up. Ann had her torch on by now and Susan wondered what was happening. 'What is it?' she said. 'A visitor downstairs. You must be dreaming, Ann.'

'That's what I want to find out,' said Ann, 'because the visitor is Santa Claus, Susan. I thought perhaps I must be dreaming, so I came to get you and the boys – because then you can tell me if I am.'

Susan got up and put on her dressing-gown. She was puzzled and astonished, and quite excited. They went to get the boys, who were very hard to wake.

'Well, if Ann's dreaming, we all must be,' said Peter, not very pleased at being woken up so suddenly. 'What's all this about a visitor downstairs? Of course Ann is dreaming. There won't be anyone there when we get down.'

But there was. Santa Claus still sat there, huge and kindly, his face redder than ever by the light of the fire. The children stood still and stared at him.

'Golly – it *is* Santa Claus,' said Peter, and gave a squeal of delight.

'Ssh!' said Susan. Ann caught her arm. 'Am I dreaming, Susan? Say I'm not! Say it's all real.'

'Well, if you're dreaming, we *all* are,' said Susan.

'I don't see that it matters whether you are dreaming or not,' said Santa Claus, shaking hands with each of them. 'It's good, whatever it is, dream or reality. How do you do? It's so nice to get a welcome like this.'

'Well, we always thought that you didn't like being seen,' said Susan. 'Children are always told to be asleep when you come.'

'Ah, I come so late in the night, you see,' said Santa Claus. 'It wouldn't do for little children to lie awake for hours – they would be very tired on Christmas day, and would get cross and naughty. Anyway, I prefer to do what I have to do quickly and secretly – though this does make a very nice change.'

'Susan, where are the biscuits?' said Ann, hopping about on one leg as she always did when she was excited. 'And can you make some cocoa? Santa Claus is thirsty.'

'Oh yes, of course I can,' said Susan, delighted. 'I'll bring a saucepan of milk in here.' She ran out and soon came back with a big saucepan of milk, a tin of cocoa, a tall jug, and a basin of sugar on a tray. She set the saucepan of milk on the fire to heat.

Benny had found the tin of biscuits and he took off the lid. Susan sent Ann to get five cups and saucers for the cocoa. Everyone felt happy and excited. This was a wonderful thing to happen in the middle of the night.

Soon the cocoa was made. Susan poured out five cups of the milky mixture, and added sugar. Then the biscuits were handed round, and everyone settled down to enjoy themselves and talk.

'Are your reindeer all right up on the cold roof?'

said Ann, hearing a soft jingle just then.

'Oh yes,' said Santa Claus. 'I always throw a rug over each of them before I come down the chimney. How nice of you to think of them.'

'Santa Claus, we've often wondered who you really are,' said Peter shyly. 'How did you get your name? Is it really Claus? And what does Santa mean? And why do you come so secretly into people's houses? How was it you began to give presents?'

'What a list of questions!' said Santa Claus, sipping his cocoa. 'I'd better tell you my own story, I think. Then you'll know all about me.'

'Oh *yes*,' said the children, together, and Benny poked the fire to make a good blaze.

'Well, to begin with, my name is not really Santa Claus,' said Santa Claus. 'My real name is Nicholas – Saint Nicholas.'

'How was it that you were called Santa Claus then?' said Ann, puzzled.

'I can tell you that,' said Santa Claus, taking another

biscuit. 'The Dutch people have always called me "San Nicolaas" which is Dutch for St Nicholas. Well, years and years ago, Dutchmen went to America, and there my name San Nicolaas was pronounced by the Americans as "Santa Claus." Say "San Nicolaas" quickly over and over again to yourselves and you will see how easily it becomes "Santa Claus."'

'San Nicolass, San Nicolaas, Sanicolaas, Sanitclaas, Santa Claus,' said the children, and saw for themselves exactly how the name Saint Nicholas or San Nicolaas became so easily the familiar one of Santa Claus.

'Yes, San Nicolaas, I see how you got your present name!' said Benny, pleased. 'I never knew that before.'

'Lots of words get changed through the years in that way,' said Santa Claus. 'I like my name of Santa Claus.'

'So do I,' said Ann. 'It suits you. Are you really a saint?'

'Yes,' said Santa Claus. 'Not that I feel like one, really. I don't believe saints do, you know. I was a bishop, away in Lycia, and I was tortured and put into prison because I believed in Jesus Christ, and His teaching. I always liked children. I was made a saint hundreds of years ago. People built a beautiful church for me in Bari – that's in Italy. Christians used to make pilgrimages there.'

'Saints help particular people, don't they?' said Benny. 'What kind of people do *you* specially help, Santa Claus – I mean, St Nicholas?'

'Well, I'm the patron saint of Russia,' said Santa Claus, drinking the last of his cocoa. 'And I'm the patron saint of travellers and sailors – and, of course, I'm the children's own saint too. I needn't tell you that.'

'No – we all know you belong to the children,' said Susan, and she poured Santa Claus out another cup of cocoa. 'Do you know, Santa Claus, our own church here is dedicated to you – it's called the Church of St Nicholas. Fancy, the church we go to on Sundays is the Church of Santa Claus!'

'Yes, I'm pleased to say I have about four hundred

churches in your country,' said Santa Claus. 'My feast is held on December 6th. That is St Nicholas's Day.'

'So it is,' said Benny, remembering that he had seen it in his diary. 'I shall always think of you now on December 6th, St Nicholas!'

'You know, years ago, the churches used to elect a boy-bishop on my feast day,' said Santa Claus. 'I used to like that. A boy was chosen from the choir to preside over the church as bishop until December 28th. He was dressed up in full bishop's robes with a mitre and a crozier, and he made a tour of the town. He blessed the people and he gave presents to all good children.'

'What a pity we don't choose boy-bishops now,' said Benny, thinking how much he would like to be one.

'Well, they do in one or two places,' said Santa Claus, 'but not nearly as often as they used to.'

'Tell us your story now, please,' said Ann. 'I do want to hear it.'

What They Did
at Miss Brown's
School

What They Did at Miss Brown's School

DECEMBER SLIPPED into the calendar and nobody noticed it, for the children were so busy making Christmas presents and seeing to their bird-table that they did not realize November had gone.

But one day John said, 'Gracious! We break up next week – and we haven't done anything special for December, Miss Brown!'

'Well, you've been very busy indeed,' said Miss Brown. 'I hardly think you could have got anything else into our time-table, John.'

'But, Miss Brown, we can't leave December out. We really *must* do something very extra-special as it's the Christmas month,' said Susan.

'Well, I hadn't forgotten, my dear,' said Miss Brown, laughing. 'But as the special thing I had planned for this month can come at the end of the term, I didn't say anything.'

'I suppose you thought we'd be so busy thinking of Christmas cakes and Christmas trees and presents that we would forget,' said Mary. 'What do you plan for us to do, Miss Brown? There's no snow, so we can't go out and find any snow-tracks as we did in January. There's nothing to do in the garden, for we've dug it up, and burnt all our rubbish.'

'And our bulbs don't want much seeing to now,' said John. 'The Roman hyacinths and narcissi are flowering beautifully.'

'I wish we could give a treat to our friends, the birds,' said Susan, watching two tits swinging on the coconut by the window.

'Well, that's just what I thought we *would* do!' said Miss Brown. 'We shall have Christmas cakes and

Christmas trees – why can't we give the birds the same treat?'

'Oooh!' said the children, delighted. 'But how can we?'

'Do you mean *buy* a cake?' asked Peter.

'And would the birds *really* like a tree hung with toys and things?' asked Mary.

'Oh, we shall have to give them a special cake and a special sort of tree,' said Miss Brown. 'For one thing, we will make the cake ourselves, tomorrow morning. I will show you how to do it.'

Well, there was great excitement the next morning, as you can imagine! When the children came to school they saw that Miss Brown had put a big bowl on one of the tables, and around it were paper bags and tins.

'What's in the bags?' said Peter.

'Look and see,' said Miss Brown. So the children looked.

'Maize meal!' said Peter, shaking out a little into his hand. 'And this bag is full of the hemp seeds we bought the other day. What are *these* seeds, Miss Brown – these little hard round seeds?'

'Those are *millet* seeds,' said Miss Brown. 'The birds love those – and in that next bag is the ordinary canary seed I give my canary. Now, will you please empty some of each bag into my bowl and mix up the seeds!'

That was a lovely thing to do. Eight hands at once mixed up the seed very thoroughly! Then Miss Brown made the children chop up brazil nuts and peanuts – all except Susan, that is, who always cut her fingers when she could, and was not allowed a sharp knife or pointed scissors. She was very upset until Miss Brown told her to go and fetch a bag of currants off the kitchen shelf and empty some into the mixed-up seed.

'Put the nuts into the bowl, too,' said Miss Brown. 'That's right. Now we have maize seed, hemp seed, millet seed, canary seed, chopped-up peanuts and brazil nuts, and currants in our mixture so far.'

'This will be a good cake!' said John, feeling

quite hungry.

'Now I must get my melted fat,' said Miss Brown, going to the schoolroom fire, where a pan was sizzling with melting dripping. She poured the hot melted fat into the bowl, and let Mary stir it with a long spoon.

'Good!' she said. 'Our cake is finished!'

'But what about cooking it?' asked Mary, in surprise.

'It doesn't need to be cooked!' said Miss Brown. 'Look, I'll just get a cloth – here is one – and empty the whole mixture into it – and tie it up tightly like this – and then we'll put it in the larder and let it dry. Then we will cut slices out of it for the birds!'

'Oh, Miss Brown, I do think that's a good idea,' said Mary. 'I shall make a cake just like this at home. It's so easy!'

'Well, be careful of the boiling fat, if you do,' said Miss Brown. 'Here is the cake all tightly wrapped up in the cloth, Mary. Go and put it at the back of my larder on an enamel plate. Next week we will give the birds a slice of their Christmas cake each day.'

'We could put berries in the next one we make, couldn't we?' said Susan. 'Wouldn't the birds like yew berries and holly berries mixed in, too?'

'Oh yes,' said Miss Brown. 'Sometimes I collect the autumn berries and dry them, and then use them for the bird cake too – but the one we have made will please the birds very much indeed.'

'And now, what about the Christmas tree?' asked John. 'I saw such a dear little tree at the greengrocer's yesterday, Miss Brown. It was ninepence.'

'That will do very well,' said Miss Brown. 'I will give you the ninepence, John, and you shall buy it for us and bring it to school yourself.'

Next morning John brought the tree along. It really was a nice little tree, with a big spike at the top. John put it into a big pot and made the earth firm around the roots.

'What are you going to hang on it?' asked Susan. 'Dolls and trains?'

Miss Brown laughed. 'No,' she said, 'I don't think the birds would enjoy those much – and nobody would be more surprised than you, Susan, if you saw a sparrow nursing a doll, or a blackbird driving a toy train.'

Susan giggled. 'Well, what *are* we going to hang on the tree?' she asked.

'Something for the birds to *eat*, of course,' said John. 'Bits of coconut would be good, wouldn't they, Miss Brown?'

'Very good,' said Miss Brown.

'And bits of bacon rind and a bone or two!' said Peter.

'And a few biscuits, perhaps!' said Mary.

'And what about threading strings of peanuts and hanging those here and there, or winding them about the branches!' cried John, getting excited.

'Oh yes – and we could spare a bit of mistletoe with berries on, for the mistle-thrush!' cried Susan. 'He likes mistletoe berries, doesn't he, Miss Brown?'

'Very much,' said Miss Brown. 'And another thing the birds love on a Christmas tree are two or three millet-seed sprays – we can buy them at two pence each – big sprays of millet seeds on a long stalk!'

Well, it wasn't long before the children got to work on their Christmas tree for the birds. Miss Brown gave Mary sixpence to buy three millet sprays, and these were tied to the branches. They were full of little hard millet seeds, beloved by the sparrows and finches.

John bought a coconut from his own money. He cut the white nut into small pieces and tied each piece to the tree, so that they hung down like toys.

Mary brought some biscuits with little holes in. She threaded a piece of cotton through one of the middle holes and hung the biscuits on the tree too.

Peter brought two small bones and some bacon rind, which he tied carefully to the branches as well. The tree was really beginning to look very full.

Then all the children threaded a string of peanuts each, driving their big needles through the shells and stringing them together. The peanuts looked wonderful hanging down from the tree. And last of all, a spray of mistletoe was tied to the top spire.

'Now our tree is finished,' said Miss Brown. 'Doesn't it look fine! We will put it out for the birds before we break up, even though Christmas is not yet here, because it will be such fun to see them all enjoying it.'

So out went the tree in the middle of the lawn – and do you know, in two or three minutes the tits and the robin had found it and were having a lovely time in it! The robin perched right at the top and sang a little song, very short and sweet. The tits attacked the coconut and the peanuts and were delighted to see so much food in one place.

Then the sparrows flew down and pecked the biscuits, and the chaffinches discovered the millet seeds. A big blackbird decided he would like a biscuit, and two starlings squabbled over a bone. It really was fun to watch the tree so full of birds.

'Could we see if our cake is ready yet?' asked Susan. 'We could give the birds a piece if it is.'

Mary was sent to fetch in the cake, still tied up in its cloth. She undid it – and there was the bird cake, quite dry and ready to be eaten. It did look nice.

'You can cut the first piece, Mary,' said Miss Brown. So Mary proudly took a knife and cut a big slice of the cake. It did look lovely with all the currants, nuts and seeds inside!

'Please could I taste just a little tiny bit of it?' begged Susan.

'Of course not, Susan,' said Miss Brown. 'You know perfectly well that no food prepared for animals or birds should be eaten by children – why, just suppose we had put yew berries into this! They would poison you!'

'It does look so nice, though,' said Susan. 'Can I put it on the bird-table, Miss Brown?'

Miss Brown said yes, so Susan put it there – and almost at once the birds found it. How they enjoyed it!

They each found something they liked in it, and pecked away at the seeds, currants, nuts and fat for all they were worth. It was a very pleasant sight to see.

'Well, Miss Brown,' said Mary, as the children watched the birds, 'each month I've thought that we did something nicer than the last – but I *really* think this month has been the best!'

'Good!' said Miss Brown. 'Well, we've had a lovely year together – and if we've learnt to understand and to love the world around us more than we did a year ago, then we have done well!'

They really did have a lovely time, didn't they? Perhaps you will be able to share the same fun each month, then you will know how much the children at Miss Brown's school enjoyed it. And now we will wish them a very happy Christmas, and say goodbye until the next year.

The Christmas Tree
Party

The Christmas Tree Party

THE CHILDREN across the road were going to have a party. Janey knew, because she had seen an enormous Christmas tree arriving there, and she had seen a most beautiful Christmas cake being taken in, too, with candles all round it!

Janey wished she knew the children across the road, but she didn't. Janey didn't go to their school, and their mother wouldn't let them play with children they didn't know. So Janey just had to watch them and wonder about them – but she did wish she knew them, and could play games with them and go to their lovely, lovely parties!

'Mummy!' she said. 'Look! The children across the road are going to have a party. I can see somebody putting lights and ornaments on the Christmas tree in the front room.'

'Horrid, stuck-up children!' said Janey's brother. 'They think themselves too good for us! I hope they have a horrid party!'

'Don't be unkind, Robin,' said Mother. 'They look very nice children to me.'

'I'm going to watch what happens,' said Janey. 'If only they don't draw their curtains I can see everything plainly. I believe they are going to have tea in the front room too – I can see someone putting a big white cloth over a long table.

Janey watched for a long time. It did seem as if the party was going to be a beautiful one! Janey counted how many chairs were round the table – sixteen! Plates of sandwiches and cakes and buns and bowls of jellies and trifles. And right in the very middle of the table was the big Christmas cake, but the candles would not be lit until teatime.

'A Christmas tree party is the very best kind of party,' said Janey to herself. 'Oh, I do believe the children's mother is going to put all the presents on the tree now!'

So she was! The tree reached almost to the ceiling, and already had dozens of lights on it, and some bright, shiny ornaments and coloured balls. Now the mother was hanging dolls and engines and books and motor-cars and all kinds of exciting toys on it. Janey felt so excited herself that she had to jump up and down on the chair she was kneeling on!

'Anyone one would think you were going to the party yourself!' said Robin grumpily. 'Can't you keep still?'

'No, I can't,' said Janey. 'It's all so exciting. Do come and watch, Robin.'

'No, thank you,' said Robin. 'If I can't go to a party I don't want to watch other people going to it!'

'They're arriving!' cried Janey. 'Here's a car

with two little girls in it. One has a blue party frock and the other has a yellow one, and they both have ribbons in their hair and blue capes. And here come two boys walking down the street with their father. And here's another car – with three children and their mother. Oh, how excited they must feel!'

Janey watched all the children run up the path and go into the house. She hoped they would go into the front room, but they didn't.

'They must be playing games before tea in the room at the back,' she told Robin. 'What fun it will be to watch them come and have tea!'

There was very little to see after that, for no one came into the front room at all. The tea was ready, and the Christmas tree was waiting with its lights twinkling. Everyone was playing musical chairs with the children in the back room.

Janey sat and looked at the house opposite, loving the firelight that shone over the tea-table, and trying to see all the presents that hung on the big Christmas tree.

And then she noticed a very peculiar thing. The Christmas tree seemed to be falling over a bit. Yes – it was certainly slanting forward. How strange!

Janey watched, half scared. The tree tilted over a little more – it seemed to be falling towards the tea-table. It would spoil all the cakes and the jellies – it would crush that beautiful Christmas cake! It must be too heavy for its tub. It was slowly falling, falling over!

'Robin! Look!' cried Janey. 'The Christmas tree is falling over! Everything will be spoilt!'

'And a good thing too,' said unkind Robin, who hated to see anyone having things he hadn't got. 'Let it fall and break everything up!'

'Oh no, no, no!' cried Janey. 'Oh no! It is too beautiful to be spoilt, and the children will be so unhappy! I shall go and tell them!'

And before Robin could say a word more the little

girl shot out of the room, out of the front door, and across the street! She banged at the door there and when the other came to open it in surprise, Janey told her why she had come.

'Your Christmas tree is falling down!' she cried. 'It's spoiling itself and the lovely tea-table! I saw it from my window. Oh, quick, come and stop it!'

She and the mother ran into the front room and were just in time to save the big Christmas tree from toppling over altogether! Nothing had been spoilt – but Janey was only just in time! The father came running in, and very soon he had the tree upright again, safely packed in its tub, and weighted down with some big stones.

'Well!' said the mother, looking at Janey. 'What a lucky thing it was for us that you were watching the tree! Thank you so much.'

'I've been watching everything,' said Janey. 'It was so exciting – seeing all the table laid with those lovely things – and watching the children come – and seeing you hang the presents on the tree. It was almost as good as coming myself. I'm glad I saved the tree for you.'

'Are you the little girl that lives over the road?' asked the mother. 'My children have often said they would like to know you. Let's run across the road to your mother and see if she will let you come to the party! One little girl hasn't come because she has a cold, so we have an empty place. It would be so nice if you could come!'

Well, think of that! Janey could hardly believe her ears! She took the mother's hand and they ran across the road. In a few ninutes Janey's mother had heard all about how Janey had saved the Christmas tree from falling on to the tea-table, and Janey was putting on her pink party frock and brushing her hair in the greatest excitement!

Robin stood and watched. How he wished he had been as kind as Janey! If only he had run across with her and saved the tree, perhaps he would have been asked too. But he had been jealous and sulky – and that never brings treats or surprises, as kindness does!

Janey went to the party, and oh, what a fine one it was! All the children were told how Janey had saved the party and they thought she was wonderful.

And what do you think Janey had from the Christmas tree? Guess! She had the beautiful fairy doll off the very top, because everyone said she ought to have the nicest present of all. Wasn't she lucky? But she really did deserve that doll, didn't she?

Now she is great friends with the children across the road, and so is Robin. They play together every Saturday and go to tea once a week. It was a good thing that Janey watched the party that afternoon, wasn't it?

The Story of
Santa Claus

A Family Christmas
Part Ten:

The Story of Santa Claus

SANTA CLAUS looked into the fire for a moment or two, remembering old, old days. Then he began his story.

'Long long ago, in the city of Myra in Lycia, there lived a poor man. He had three daughters growing up in his house, laughing and chattering just as you do.

'The three girls used to talk of what they would do when they were married. Their father was so poor that they had few clothes, not enough to eat, and very few good times. It would be nice to marry and have a home of their own, and husbands who could give them what they wanted.

'"I shall have a fine house and a lovely garden," said one.

'"I shall have plenty of good food on my table and lovely clothes," said another.

'"I shall have beautiful children, and I shall ask our father to come and stay with me and be happy," said the third.

'So they talked of the happy time they hoped they would have when they were all grown-up.

'But, in those days, nobody wanted to marry girls without any money. Only those girls whose fathers could give them plenty of money were likely to make good marriages.

'The father of the three girls was so poor that he could hardly have provided for one girl – and he had three. The poor man did not know what to do.

'"I must try to marry them to good men, who will not ask for a great deal of money," thought the father. So, when his daughters were grown up, he tried to find men who would marry them, and give them homes, without asking a great deal of money with each girl.

'But alas, however much he tried, he could not find one man who would offer to marry one of his daughters. The time went on, and still the three girls lived in his poor home, feeling sad and miserable because there seemed no chance of having homes of their own.

'"All our friends are married now," they said to one another. "Some have children to love. Only we are not married. What is to happen to us?"

'Their father grew so poor that he thought he would have to sell his daughters as slaves. The girls cried bitterly when they heard this. How terrible to be sold! What a miserable life they had to look forward to!

'Now one day word was brought to me that these three girls were very unhappy. I knew them, and I was sorry for them. I could not bear to think that they would be sold, and would never know the happiness of a home and children of their own.

'But I could not go to their father and offer him money for I knew he would not accept a gift like that. It would have to be done secretly. So, one night, when it was very dark, and no one could see me, I stole to this poor man's house. With me I had three purses full of money. There was one for each of the poor girls.

'As I walked softly outside the house I could hear the girls weeping. There was a high wall round the house, and I thought I would throw the purses over it. Then, in the morning they would be found, and, as there were three, the girls would guess that some secret friend had thrown them over for their own use.

'So I threw one purse after another over the high wall. I heard them fall with a clank to the ground. Then I hurried away in the night, my heart glad because I had been able to save three people from a life of misery.

'In the morning the girls looked out of the window and they saw the three purses lying outside.

'"What are those?" they wondered, and one went

out to see. She picked up the heavy purses, and they jingled with money. She rushed indoors, crying loudly for joy, "There is money here, much money!"

'The girls opened the three purses and found the same amount of money in each one. "There are *three* purses," they said, "and we are three girls. So one must be for each of us. Let us tell our father!"

'Their father was overjoyed when he saw so much money. "Now I shall not have to sell you," he said. "You can marry good men, and lead happy lives of your own."

'So the three girls were soon happily married, and went to good homes of their own. They never forgot the night when the money came over the wall, and I know they often spoke of it.

'This secret giving of presents made me very happy. They did not know it was I who had given them the money, so they could not thank me, and I didn't want to be thanked. So, after that, I again and again gave presents in secret to those who needed my gifts.

'And, even to this day, I do the same thing as you know. I come secretly to children, I give them presents without letting them see me do it, I creep away because I don't want any thanks. No one sees me – but tonight you have caught me, and here I am, telling you my story!'

The children had listened to Santa Claus telling his kindly tale, and had not made a movement. So that was how the custom began of giving presents secretly at Christmas-time. A kindly secret deed had made St Nicholas so happy, all those many years ago, that he had continued with his secret kindness, so that, to this very night, children all over the world hung up stockings for his secret gifts!

'How strange old customs are, with their histories reaching so far back into the past,' said Susan. 'Our life isn't all in the present, is it, Santa Claus? It is made up of thousands of bits of the past, old things that happened, old names, old habits. The past and the present and the future all belong to one another.'

'Of course,' said Santa Claus. 'And we ought to live in them all, not just thoughtlessly in the present. We ought to know our past, and we ought to plan for our future. Then the present would always be worth living in.'

Ann thought the talk was getting rather solemn. She squeezed Santa Claus's hand.

'It was a lovely story,' she said, 'and it was just like you to do such a kind thing. I'd like to hug you for all your secret kindnesses, Santa Claus.'

'Well, I don't mind if you do,' said Santa Claus beaming. So Ann hugged him, and he chuckled deep down in his beard.

'I always did like children,' he said. 'There's a lot more sense in them than in most grown-ups, and it's a pity you lose it as you grow. Well, well – I suppose I must be going.'

'No – don't go yet!' begged the children.

'My reindeer will be getting restless,' said Santa Claus. 'My sleigh and reindeer were an idea of the old Norsemen, you know, and a very good one, I think. My sleigh runs so lightly because, so the Norsemen said, it was built in Fairyland. It's easy to get about in it.'

'Why don't you give presents secretly on your own day, December 6th?' asked Peter.

'I used to,' said Santa Claus, 'but somehow people thought that Christmas was a better time for gifts, and I think it is myself. So I come on Christmas Eve, as you know, and you find my presents on Christmas Day – and other people's too, of course.'

'I suppose our Christmas festival began with the birthday of the Baby Jesus,' said Susan. 'Nearly two thousand years ago.'

'Oh, December 25th was a holiday or festival long long before that,' said Santa Claus. 'Many peoples held feasts at this time of the year, even the Britons, before the birth of Christ. Then the early Christians took many of the old pagan ideas and customs, and used them in their own religion.'

'Does everyone now celebrate Christmas Day on December 25th?' asked Benny. 'Was it always kept on that day?'

'Oh no,' said Santa Claus. 'For some time, after Jesus Christ was born, the church did not celebrate Christmas at all, and then later on, the date was fixed for December 25th in the West, but January 6th in the East. It wasn't until a good many years had gone by that Christmas was celebrated on the same day by nearly everyone.'

'We have a cousin in Scotland,' said Ann, 'and do you know, she says that their great day there is not Christmas Day, but New Year's Day. Isn't that strange? Why is it?'

'Ah, I can tell you that,' said Santa Claus. 'About three hundred years ago, when Christmas was becoming rather a wild and unrestrained feast, many people were disgusted, and said that Christmas should be a sacred day, not a wild holiday. So Parliament forbade the keeping of Christmas Day as a feast or holiday. But it was not very long before the people were allowed once more to keep it as a real holiday. All but the Scottish people once again kept December 25th as a festival – but the Scots would not, and to this day they keep New Year's Day as their great holiday, and not Christmas Day.'

'I see,' said Peter. 'Now I know why Cousin Jeanie doesn't keep Christmas, but gets excited about New Year's Day. I never knew that before – and she didn't either, because I asked her. I'll write and tell her.'

'You won't know much about *this* Christmas Day, if I don't go soon!' said Santa Claus, getting up out of his chair. 'You'll all be so sleepy that you won't wake up until the afternoon – and you'll miss the pudding and everything!'

'We shall be awake all right!' said Susan, with a laugh. 'Are you really going, Santa Claus? It has been lovely to hear your story and talk to you.'

'Just as nice for me,' said Santa Claus, beaming all over his ruddy, cheerful face. 'Listen to those reindeer of mine – getting quite impatient!'

The children could hear the stamping of hooves on the snow-covered roof, and the jingle of bells. Yes, it was time for Santa Claus to go!

'Now you hop upstairs as quickly as you can,' said Santa, pulling out his enormous watch again. 'Go along. You can watch out of the window for me, and see my sleigh going off.'

The children said goodnight, wished Santa Claus a happy Christmas, and went upstairs, pleased and happy. What a fine time they had had!

Ann pushed the bottle of sweets into his hand and gave him another hug when she said goodbye. She had quite lost her heart to the sturdy old man.

'I'm glad you're the children's saint,' she said. 'I'm glad to have a saint like you for my own. Goodnight!'

The four children watched at the window for Santa Claus to go. They saw and heard nothing for quite a while. 'I hope he hasn't got stuck in the chimney,' said Ann.

But, after some time, they heard the jingling of bells and harness, and off the roof slid the big sleigh, borne through the air as lightly as a feather. The moon shone out just then, and Santa Claus waved to the watching children at the window. Then he disappeared into the night, only a faint jingling coming on the air.

The children went back to bed. 'It hasn't been a dream, has it?' said Ann to Susan. 'Say it hasn't, Susan.'

'Well – I don't feel it has,' said Susan, 'but it really has been extraordinary, hasn't it? I'm very sleepy now. Goodnight, Ann.'

Santa Claus
Gets Busy

Santa Claus
Gets Busy

SANTA CLAUS was having a little snooze in his armchair on the afternoon before Christmas Day, when someone came banging at his door.

'Who is it? Didn't I say nobody was to . . . ?' began Santa Claus, waking up with a jump. A little servant ran into the room.

'Santa Claus! Your reindeer are ill! Sneezing their heads off! They can't possibly take your sleigh tonight. You'll have to put off Christmas Eve.'

'Don't be silly!' said Santa, and he leaped up at once. 'Nobody can put off Christmas Eve. I'll come and have a look at the reindeer.'

But when he saw them he knew they couldn't pull his sleigh. They could hardly stand. He stared at them in dismay. '*Now* what am I to do? Can't disappoint all those millions of children!'

'Go in a helicopter,' said the stable-man. 'It's easy to land on roofs in that.'

Santa Claus snorted like a reindeer. 'A helicopter! What next? I don't go in for these new-fashioned things. I'm old-fashioned and I like reindeer for Christmas Eve. Now – where in the world can I get some?'

'I saw some once in the London zoo,' said the stable-man, wiping a reindeer's nose for him. 'Not so good as these. Still, they might do. You'd have to ask the keeper though.'

'I will!' said Santa Claus. 'Get him on the telephone at once.' So, to the enormous astonishment of the reindeer's keeper at the zoo, Santa Claus talked down the telephone to him, and suggested that he should lend him four of his best reindeer in a few hours' time.

'Don't be funny,' growled the keeper, who didn't believe in Santa Claus. 'I don't like this kind of joke.'

Santa Claus was angry. 'What's your name?' he snapped. 'John Robins? Wait a minute. I'll look you up in my Christmas book. Yes, here you are – twenty-five years ago you were a little boy living in Jasmine Cottage, Ardale. That right?'

'Er – yes – that's right,' said the keeper, puzzled.

'And one Christmas you badly wanted a toy farm and called up the chimney to ask me for it, didn't you?' said Santa Claus. 'And what's more, I heard you, and brought it. I put the farm at the end of your bed and filled your stocking with the animals and the farmer. Do you remember? *Now* will you believe I'm Santa Claus, and lend me four of your reindeer?'

By this time the keeper was so puzzled and scared that he was ready to agree to anything. 'Well, listen,' said Santa Claus. 'Get them out at once. Say one word into their ears – annimal-oolipatahmekaroo. Got it? Repeat it after me. It's a magic word that all reindeer know. I'll send a messenger with some fly-paint for their heels.'

'Fly-paint?' said the keeper, faintly.

'Yes – fly-paint to make them gallop up into the air,' said Santa Claus, impatiently. 'I'll send them back safely when I've finished with them. Thanks very much.' He slammed down the telephone receiver and blew out his cheeks. 'Done it! Where's Pip? Send him straight to the zoo with the paint for the reindeers' hooves.'

In two hours four magnificent reindeer came galloping through the evening sky to the castle of Santa Claus. The keeper had groomed them beautifully, and had even polished their antlers with furniture polish. He felt as if he were in a dream as he whispered 'annimaloolipatahmekaroo,' but when he saw the reindeer at last galloping up into the air, he couldn't help feeling pleased and excited. 'I must tell my little boy,' he said. 'He won't believe me, but I really must tell him.'

The toys were all ready packed into Santa Claus's sack. They made their usual yearly grumble about being too squashed for words, but Santa took no notice of that. At exactly the right moment he rose into the air, his great sleigh pulled easily along by the four zoo reindeer. Bells jingled madly, and Santa Claus held on to his hood, and pulled at the reins.

'Hey! Not so fast! There's a speed-limit for reindeer.'

They slowed down a little. They were proud and excited, and it was a long time since they had had a real gallop. They were good and intelligent animals, and only made one mistake. That was when one of them accidentally put his hoof through a sky-light on a roof, and broke it. Santa Claus's own reindeer never did a thing like that. They were too well-trained.

'Never mind, never mind!' said Santa Claus. 'I'll put a special window-mending outfit into the child's stocking here. He'll enjoy that. Whoa now! You're just too lively for anything!'

Not a child was forgotten that night, and Santa Claus did the whole journey in record time, because the reindeer were so fresh, and so keen to show what they could do. They took him back to his castle at last, and he got down from the sleigh, his sack empty, tired out. He patted the reindeer, and gave them each a nose-bag full of reindeer moss.

'Hey, Pip!' he called. 'Take them back when they've had a feed and a rub-down. Good creatures they are. That keeper ought to be proud of them. Oh, and Pip, slip down the keeper's chimney, will you, and put this into his little boy's stocking. I didn't think of it when I was there.'

He gave Pip four beautiful little toy reindeer pulling a sleigh with a tiny figure of himself driving it. 'And see that you wipe the fly-paint from their hooves *properly*,' he said. 'We don't want to hear of reindeer gadding about above the zoo next summer. Though I daresay they would make a lot of money giving children rides through the air! Get along, now, Pip, and return the reindeer.'

Pip went off, riding the first reindeer, and leading the others on a rein. He set them all safely down in their quarters at the zoo. He slipped down the keeper's chimney and left Santa Claus's present in the child's stocking. Then he took a duster from his pocket and went to rub off the fly-paint from the hooves.

But wait a minute – hey, Pip! Come back again. You've forgotten one of the reindeer – he's still got the paint on his hooves. But Pip's gone. Well, well – that means a bit of excitement at the zoo one day next year. I hope I'm there to see it!

Christmas Day

A Family Christmas
Part Eleven:

Christmas Day

ANN AWOKE first on Christmas morning. The clock began to strike in the hall downstairs as she awoke. She counted the strokes – one, two, three, four, five, six, seven.

'Oh good,' said Ann, 'seven o'clock – and Christmas Day. I can look at my presents. But I forgot – of course Santa Claus didn't leave us any last night. He didn't come upstairs at all.'

She switched on the light, for it was still quite dark outside – and to her great amazement she saw that her stocking was quite full of toys. A lovely doll, with curly hair and a blue bow, peeped out of the top.

Susan's stocking was full too. How strange. Ann leaned over to Susan's bed and shook her.

'Susan! Wake up. Santa Claus has filled our stockings – but *when* did he do it?'

Susan awoke – and then there came the sound of voices and laughter from the boys' room.

'I say, you girls. Our stockings are full. Are yours? We'll bring ours in.'

There was the patter of feet, and Benny and Peter came in, carrying stockings that were almost bursting with toys.

'Look!' said Peter, pulling out a big top. 'Heaps of things. Now *when* did old Santa Claus come and fill our stockings? That's what I would like to know. We were with him all the time he was here. He couldn't possibly have slipped upstairs without us seeing him.'

'*I* know when he filled them,' said Ann, suddenly. 'When we were all watching and waiting for him at the window. Don't you remember how we thought he was a very long time – and I wondered if he had got stuck in the chimney? *That's* when he came to fill them.'

'Of course!' said Benny. 'We were all pressing our noses to the pane, and watching for him – and he was there behind us, quietly stuffing toys into our stockings, in his usual kindly, secret way – so we couldn't thank him.'

'Dear old Santa Claus,' said Ann. 'That's just like him. Look at this doll's chest-of-drawers in my stocking – isn't it sweet?'

Mother came in to the room, smiling. 'I heard all the noise,' she said. 'Happy Christmas, dears!'

'Happy Christmas, Mummy!' said the children, and kissed her. Then Ann told the great news.

'Mummy – Santa Claus came in the night – and we all went down and saw him – and he told us his story, and lots of other things too.'

'You dreamed it,' said Mother, laughing.

'But Mummy – we must *all* have dreamt the same dream then,' said Ann. 'We did have such a nice time.

The Yule-log was still burning – and we ate up all the biscuits.'

'What nonsense you talk,' said Mother. 'Now get back into bed, or you'll catch cold.'

'Christmas Day at last,' said Peter, cuddling into Ann's bed to open his presents with Ann. 'It was such a long time coming – and it goes so quickly when it's here.'

'Christmas presents – and Christmas pudding – and a turkey – and crackers – and Christmas trees. What a lovely time it is,' said Ann, pulling a gorgeous pencil out of her stocking. 'Just look at this, Peter.'

'I'm jolly glad somebody began a festival at Christmas-time,' said Benny. 'It's one of the best old customs I know. I hope it will go on forever.'

It was a lovely Christmas Day for the four children, and for the grown-ups too. The snow was still on the ground. The Yule-log was actually still alight in the hearth and Mother broke off a bit to keep till the next Christmas, so that she might light the next log with it.

The pudding was brought in, all on fire, because Daddy had put brandy on it and then set light to it. 'Another old habit!' he said, 'and a most amusing one too. See how it burns.'

It was a delicious pudding. Ann had the silver thimble, and the other three had a silver coin each, so that was lucky.

After tea the Christmas tree was lighted in the hall. How lovely it looked, as it stood there, its candles burning with a soft, glowing light. The ornaments glittered and swung, and the frost and tinfoil glistened like real frost and ice. The star at the top shone over the fairy doll, who looked down smiling, just as she had done for so many Christmases.

'I love Christmas,' said Ann, dancing round the tree. 'And I love it even more now I know such a lot about it. I wish somebody would write a book, and put into it all the things we know about Christmas time.'

So I have – and here it is. And now we must leave Ann and her family with the lighted Christmas tree.

The candles are almost burnt down. Christmas is nearly over.

But it will come again with all its love and kindliness, the birthday of the little Jesus born so many hundreds of years ago, and we will say once more, with the angels,

'GLORY TO GOD IN THE HIGHEST; AND ON EARTH PEACE, GOODWILL TOWARDS MEN!'

The Christmas
Tree Fairy

The Christmas
Tree Fairy

THERE WAS once a hill which was covered with fir trees. They were fine trees, tall and straight, and always dressed in green, for they did not throw down their leaves in autumn as other trees did. They were evergreens.

'We must grow as tall as we can!' whispered the firs to one another. 'Tall, tall and straight.'

'I want to be the mast of a ship, then I shall always feel the wind rocking me,' said one fir.

'I want to be a telegraph post,' said another tree. 'Then all day and night I shall hear messages whispering along the wires!'

'I would like to be a scaffolding pole, put up when new houses are built,' said a third fir tree. 'I am so very, very tall.'

So the trees talked to one another – all but one small tree, which hadn't grown at all. The winter wind had once uprooted it, and it had nearly died. The woodman had replanted it, but it had never grown. It was a tiny tree, sad because it could no longer talk to its brothers.

'They are so high above me that they would not even hear my voice!' thought the little fir tree.

It was frightened when the woodman came round. It knew that the other trees were proud to know they would be masts of ships or something grand and useful – but what use would such a tiny tree be?

'One day I shall be chopped down, and made into firewood,' said the fir to itself. 'I am no use at all!'

And one morning, sure enough, the woodman came and saw the tiny tree. He didn't chop it down, but he dug it up. The little tree was sad. 'Now, this is the end of me,' it thought.

To its great surprise, it was planted in a tub, which was painted bright red. And then all kinds of strange things happened to it!

The woodman's wife hung strands of tinsel on its boughs. She put bits of cotton-wool here and there to make it look as if snow had fallen. She took bright shining glass balls and tied them to the dark little branches.

'The tree is looking lovely already!' she said. 'How pleased the children will be!'

Then she fastened twenty small and beautifully coloured candles, red, pink, yellow, blue and green, all over the tree. She tied a pretty fairy doll on to the top spike. She hung toys here and there. The tree was so astonished that it hardly knew what to think.

On Christmas Day the mother gave the little tree to her children. They clapped their hands in joy.

'Mother! Mother! It's a Christmas tree! Oh,

Mother, it's the loveliest tree we've ever, ever had! Isn't it beautiful!'

The little fir tree was glad. It was happy to give pleasure to so many people. 'Even if I am used for firewood now, I shan't mind!' it thought.

But after Christmas the woodman took the tree from its tub, and planted it in the garden round the cottage. 'It's just right for a Christmas tree!' he said. 'We'll have it for our Christmas tree every year!'

Wasn't that good luck for the little tree? I do hope you get one just like it for Christmas Day.

Acknowledgements

All efforts have been made to seek necessary permissions.

The stories in this collection first appeared in the following publications:

'A Family Christmas' was first published as *The Christmas Book* by Macmillan in 1944.

The extract from 'What They Did as Miss Brown's School' was first published as part of *Enid Blyton's Book of the Year* by Evans Brothers in 1941.

'In Santa Claus's Castle' first appeared in *Enid Blyton's Sunny Stories*, issue 536, June 1952.

'The Lost Presents' first appeared in *Enid Blyton's Snowdrop Storybook*, published by John Gifford, 1952.

'Santa Claus Gets a Shock' first appeared in *Enid Blyton's Sunny Stories*, issue 154, 1939.

'A Week Before Christmas' first appeared in *Enid Blyton's Treasury*, published by Evans Brothers in 1947.

'The Christmas Tree Aeroplane' first appeared in *The Second Holiday Book*, published by Sampson Low in 1947.

'A Hole in Santa's Sack' first appeared in *Enid Blyton's Sunny Stories*, issue 49, 1937.

'The Tiny Christmas Tree' first appeared in *Enid Blyton's Sunny Stories*, issue 256, 1941.

'What Happened on Christmas Eve' first appeared in *The Eighth Holiday Book*, published by Sampson Low in 1953.

'The Little Reindeer Bell' first appeared in *Enid Blyton's Magazine*, issue 24, 1956.

'The Very-Full Stocking' first appeared in *Enid Blyton's Sunny Stories*, issue 206, 1940.

'Santa Claus Gets Busy' first appeared in *Enid Blyton's Sunny Stories*, issue 446, 1948.

'The Christmas Tree Fairy' first appeared in *The Enid Blyton Holiday Book*, published by Sampson Low in 1947.

'The Little Christmas Tree' first appeared in *Five Minute Tales*, published by Methuen in 1933.

'The Christmas Tree Party' from *Tricky the Goblin and other stories*, published by Macmillan in 1950.